AN **ABDU**

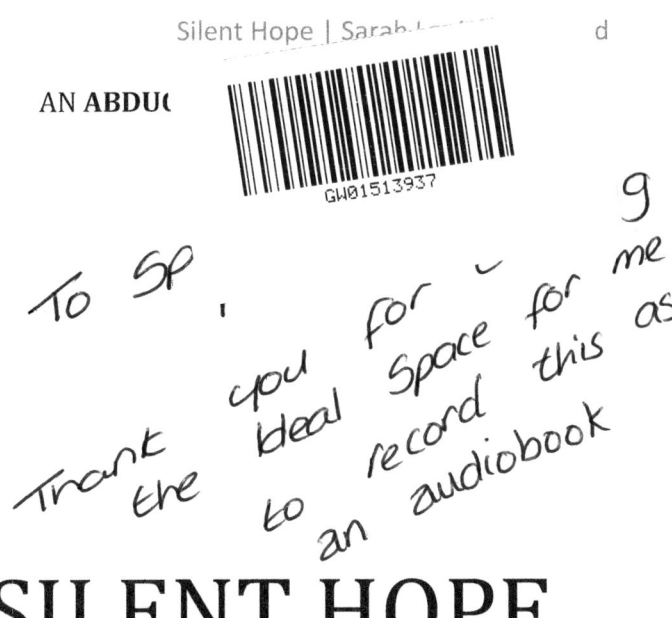

To SP,

Thank you for
the ideal space for me
to record this as
an audiobook 9

SILENT HOPE

WOULD YOU BE MISSED?

Rosmond
xxx

Sarah Louise Rosmond

Copyright

Copyright © 2022 Sarah Louise Rosmond

All rights reserved.

Although this book is based on a true story, the characters and events portrayed in this book are fictitious. Any resemblance or similarities to real persons, living or dead, is coincidental and not intended by the author.

No part of this book may be reproduced, or stored in a retrieval system, or transmitted in any form or by any means, electronic, mechanical, photocopying, recording or otherwise, without express written permission from the author and/or publisher.

ISBN – 9798325479854

Copyright © Cover design Sarah Louise Rosmond (Canva)

Printed in the United Kingdom

First printed November 2022 under the pseudonym Willow Downs

Introduction

Siobhan Everdeen was your typical teenage girl growing up in Manchester, England. She was smart and usually pretty streetwise, which you needed to be growing up in Wythenshawe. She was a confident girl, especially when running about with her mates. The only problem as far as Siobhan was concerned was her family life sucked. An abusive drunken father and a victimised mother, Siobhan found herself rebelling at the age of thirteen. Secret boyfriends, house parties and drunken mistakes were some of the things she got up to when she was allowed that taste of freedom.

Siobhan was out with a group of lads when the fateful afternoon happened, all because she wanted to rebel against her father's ridiculous rules. That became a decision she lived to regret after she was abducted in broad daylight, in front of her friends.

Held captive and the fear of being sold to a sex trafficking ring, Siobhan was almost ready to give up on everything and end it all. That was until someone else's life became her main reason for living.

Table of Contents

Copyright 2

Introduction 3

CHAPTER ONE – Siobhan Everdeen..............................8

CHAPTER TWO – Dark desperation 30

CHAPTER THREE – Entrapment 101 47

CHAPTER FOUR – Rotting corpse 62

CHAPTER FIVE – What about the baby?.....................81

CHAPTER SIX – The escape artist................................93

CHAPTER SEVEN – My getaway.................................107

CHAPTER EIGHT – My new home 119

CHAPTER NINE – Four months later 134

CHAPTER TEN – Then there were two......................144

CHAPTER ELEVEN – A little taste of freedom 154

CHAPTER TWELVE – A little bundle of Hope 159

CHAPTER THIRTEEN – Eight months later 166

CHAPTER FORTEEN – Hope Everdeen, Aged 3 172

CHAPTER FIFTEEN – Something had to change........179

CHAPTER SIXTEEN – Birthday girl 185

CHAPTER SEVENTEEN – Planning for the future 194

CHAPTER EIGHTEEN – With Hope comes Freedom..206

CHAPTER NINETEEN – Finally Free 212

Hope's Interview 222

CHAPTER TWENTY – Proving myself 225

CHAPTER TWENTY-ONE – Disappearing Darren.......238

CHAPTER TWENTY-TWO – The Investigation 248

CHAPTER TWENTY-THREE – The Verdict 252

About the Author 260

Would you be missed?

Siobhan Everdeen felt invisible…

Lightly based on a true story

CHAPTER ONE – Siobhan Everdeen

It was a normal sunny day in Bench Hill, a small council estate in the centre of Wythenshawe. I was with a group of lads who all lived near my house, and we were playing a game of football on the schools playing field. Kelvin attended Bench Hill primary years previously so even though we knew we were trespassing every time we had a kick around, we convinced ourselves that having a past pupil with us was a good enough excuse to be on the private property. It was a normal Saturday afternoon, and I had been ordered to be home by three o'clock otherwise my dad would have gone straight through me, and I knew better than to be even a minute late, otherwise I would be severely punished.

To say I didn't enjoy family life was an understatement and I hated that I had such a strict upbringing, but my father used to be a drill sergeant in the army before he married my mother, and it was something that was unfortunately deeply rooted in him. My father was a classic bully, but he'd use the army as an excuse with everyone for his lack of empathy and not to mention, his extremely short fuse. Especially when it came to his own family. The man clearly had some form of OCD as well and didn't he make sure we all knew about it.

In our home, my mother and I would be ordered about from the second we'd wake up in the morning. My father would expect me to make my bed within his specified period of time, which was usually around two minutes, unless he was in one of his shitty moods and then I'd be lucky if I had thirty seconds to make my stupid bed. At night I'd attempt to sleep as still as possible, the make the job a little easier the next morning. Dad would then give us kids exactly ten minutes to get washed and changed and to meet him in the kitchen, if we were even a second late, that would mean no cereal that day and we'd have to wait for school dinners before being fed. I liked my food, so I was always ready on time, but my little brother wasn't so punctual. For months I helped Adam get dressed and we had a system that worked, but Dad got wind of it and tried to say we were being sly and trying to defy him. We weren't, we were just working as a team. We weren't allowed teams in our house, dad made sure of that and eventually he done everything in his power to keep Adam and I separate, as much as possible in a three bedroomed house.

Our father was relentless and told us, all too often, his stupid little stories about his time in the army and he'd take pleasure in reminding us that we'd be expected to do the tasks he set for us, on a daily basis, if we ever done the B.A.R.B test for the army. I think he thought he was training us up ready to enrol. I had no intention of ever joining the army, but I wouldn't have dared to tell him that.

As soon as breakfast was finished with, if you were lucky enough to be fed, that was, my dad would order us back upstairs while our mother cleaned up our mess and done the dishes. A few minutes later and he'd enter our rooms. I was expected to stand quietly at the bottom of my bed while he ran a meter length stick of bamboo down the middle of my blankets. He would do this so that he could see if I had pulled my blanket tight enough at the corners, if I hadn't, then the fabric would gather under the stick and my bedding would move.

Sounds a little harsh, doesn't it?

The real harshness would come if or when my blanket did move. Personally, I think my dad got off on the fact that if his family didn't match up to his ridiculous standards, he could at least punish us the way he wanted to. I dreaded that bamboo stick, and he knew it. My dad would often use the bamboo cane on me, rather than on my bed. Whipping me across my back end until the point he would make me bleed and at times I was so sore and bruised, I'd be unable to sit down for days on end. The man showed no remorse, not matter how severe the punishment was, he'd tell me it was my own fault, because I was the eldest and therefore I needed to be made an example of. I had been ordered to make my bed this way for over three years, so luckily for me, I had managed to get my bed making skills down to a fine art. My dad hated that I was so good at sticking to his rules so much so, that he'd threaten me that he could be a hell of a lot worse, and to wait until I was older before I got smug about it. He often warned me that as soon as I turned sixteen, I would be expected to do the same mundane jobs as my mother. We rarely ever saw our mother; she was always cleaning a useless car part until it was gleaming or polishing the floor for the hundredth time. My father had no use for the stupid bits of metal, but he still forced my mum out into the garage to polish the same item repeatedly, just because he could.

My mother unfortunately, acted like a frail woman, too scared to ever answer my father back and far too quiet to ever be heard anyway, it was like our dad had silenced her. I hated to think about how he must've treated her in the past for her to be so muted. The only time I'd hear her speak, would be a whisper because my father apparently hated her voice. Not as much as I hated his. The only other time we would see her was at dinner time, when she'd be allowed to sit and eat her dinner with the rest of us. Although as soon as she'd finished eating, she'd be sent straight back into the kitchen to tidy up. I decided from an early age, that if that was what married life was like, I was happy to stay on my own forever. I felt for my mother but at the same time, I'd wished she had more of a backbone, then we wouldn't have had to live with him, she deserved better, we all did, but I think the poor woman had been conditioned so much that she just accepted that was how our lives were meant to be. Well, I knew as soon as I was old enough, I would be out of there in a flash.

I couldn't stand being at home, and you can surely understand why.

So, as I was saying, the group of us were playing football on the school playing field when Kelvin noticed a white van parked on the school's car park. Personally, I thought nothing of it and wanted to carry on playing football, but I noticed a man clambering out of the van, he shouted something before walking to the back of the van and opening back doors. Paul, Kelvin, and Mitch all ran over towards the car park, but I stayed where I was and carried on kicking the ball back and forth to John.

John and I had been secretly seeing each other so it was nice to get a few sacred minutes alone with him. Well, it was, until he opened his big mouth.

"I really enjoyed last weekend." he said smiling at me.

I felt awkward as hell, as John forcefully kicked the ball back in my direction. I was grateful for the little run to fetch the ball because I wanted the ground to swallow me up. John made me feel embarrassed and I was ashamed, the last thing I wanted to do was have a conversation about it all, especially while we were out with the rest of the group. It wasn't John's fault, but I was annoyed and frustrated that he'd even mentioned the previous weekend. He was talking about the weekend before, when I was staying over at Nancy's house, which I have to add, never happened usually. Sleepovers were forbidden in my house and the chance of myself staying out at a mates, was very slim but that afternoon my father was in a good mood as he'd won big on the horses, he really shocked me when he'd agreed to me staying out, overnight as long as I was home by ten the next day. I wasn't going to wait for him to change his mind, so withing ten minutes, I was out of the house and walking the twenty minutes to Nancy's house. I thought we were having a girly night, but Nancy had other ideas and she'd invited John and Chris over to join us. I didn't know that her parents were going to be away that weekend at a fancy party and weren't due home until the Sunday evening. It had been amazing to have the house to ourselves, we all felt like adults, even though we were only in third year of secondary school.

Nancy and Chris were the only people who knew about mine and John's relationship and I was hoping to keep it that way. My dad would have gone mental if he knew I was seeing a boy, and I'd would have been worried for John's safety if it ever became public knowledge. I wasn't ashamed of John, he was a good-looking boy, but I knew the rules and boys were well and truly forbidden. That night I was feeling free, rebelling against my father and that evening after drinking alcohol for the first time, I decided it would be a brilliant, grown-up idea to lose my virginity with John. I wanted to lose my virginity one day, but I instantly regretted the way it had happened.

Nancy and I had been drinking her mum's vodka for a good hour before the lads arrived. My best mate had already warned me that she was going to be leaving me on my own with John so we could have some quality time together, but really, it was because she wanted to get laid herself. Nancy had lost her virginity the year before so her and Chris were at it like rabbits at every given opportunity. Which could be a little uncomfortable when you were all sat chilling at the local kiddy park, and the two of them would start making out, not caring who was present. The way Nancy saw it, if we didn't want to see what they were both up to, we could look the other way. Pity we couldn't shield our ears just as well.

John and I had only been seeing each other for three months but had I not been drinking spirits; I am certain I would have said no to him when he asked if he could go down on me. That led to more and before I knew it, we were laid naked on my best friends bedroom floor, and we'd just had sex. It was okay, but not how I expected it to feel. Nancy raved on about how much she enjoyed sex, but it was clumsy and uncomfortable, and I honestly didn't understand the appeal.

John mentioning it to me and saying the words aloud had me panicking on the spot, so instead of kicking the ball back to my secret boyfriend, I picked it up, turned on my heels and ran over to see what caught the other lad's attention. I needed to get out of that conversation as quickly as possible because I felt ashamed of my actions, but how could I have told John that. The boy acted like he was in love with me, and he believed it was the next step in our relationship. I on the other hand, didn't agree in the slightest and I even contemplated ending things with him before they got any more complicated. I didn't want to hurt him, but keeping him a secret, wasn't easy and I didn't believe the boy was worth all the hassle that would come from it.

I made my way over to the rest of our group; and as usual they didn't even notice me, because they were too busy talking between themselves. To make myself known, I threw the ball straight at Kelvin's head. He turned and looked at me in disbelief.

"Seriously, don't be a dick, titch! We're trying to sus out what that strange man is doing in the back of his van."

"Looks dodgy if you ask me" I said, reaching the rest of the group. "sorry about your face Kel." John I noticed was in close pursuit behind me.

Kelvin nodded at me, "It didn't hurt, cause you throw like a girl." He joked.

"I am a girl."

"What's going on?" John asked.

"That guy just said we can have some free sweets" Paul smiled.

"What's the catch?" I shouted over towards the parked vehicle. I was a lot more vocal when I wasn't around my own family. My mates saw my loudmouth side, every so often. It was an act, I wasn't really all that confident but if you'd asked my mates, they would have told you the opposite. A middle-aged man was stood at the back of the van, and he told us we could all have free sweets and all we had to do was let all the other kids in the estate know about his mobile sweet van.

Sounded fair enough to me.

We'd get free sweets for a bit of free advertising. Win, win!
Normally I'd not be allowed to eat sweet things, dad would complain that all the sugar would ruin my teeth so when all the other kids in the street went off to the ice cream van, I usually stayed on the square. I lied and told the group that I didn't like ice cream, but I had no idea whether or not I liked the stuff because I'd never tried it.

However, at this point I had already broken all my dad's rules, especially when I decided to have sex, so I didn't see the harm in adding to my list of sins. I wanted to try sweets more than anything in the world and at the time it seemed like the best chance I would have. I would have been lynched if I'd be caught at the shop, so the sweet van was ideal.

I looked down at my watch, with just over an hour before I needed to be home, I decided I would have enough time to eat the sweets and get rid of any evidence before heading back, I had plenty of time to spare.

"I'm up for it." I smiled, but Kelvin told me he didn't trust the man, one bit.

"What if it is poisoned or summit?" he worried, but I just laughed at him.

Kelvin was known to get a little paranoid at times, so I took no notice. The only thing that was standing in the way of me trying sweets for the first time was a big six-foot metal fence, which I knew I could climb easy, but John being so thoughtful offered to give me a hand over. I accepted as he crouched down into his karate stance ready to take my weight. I placed my foot into his cupped hands and John used his own strength to push me up high enough to climb over.

Next to jump over the fence was Kelvin, followed closely by Mitch. John had made some silly excuse about staying where he was to keep an eye out, and I couldn't help but wonder if it was because I had just dismissed him, but in the same breath, I wasn't about to stress over his feelings too much. I wasn't sure what he even meant to me anymore, sleeping with him put a wedge between us, rather than bringing us closer together, it done the opposite. John could be in a mood with me, I didn't care. My mouth was watering at the thought of those free sweets.

The three of us made our way over to the van. The man was still standing near the back of the vehicle. Seeing him stood there had me feeling a little uneasy, there was something about the bloke that didn't sit well with me. I thought he looked a little dodgy with his muddy black trousers and worn-out brown leather jacket, but each to their own. We approached the van, which was now only metres away when the man shouted over to us.

"Only one at a time." I turned to look at Mitch who just shrugged his shoulders at me. "Not enough room for all of you, and I need to see what sweets you are having." The strange man said.

Kelvin walked over first, I didn't see him going into the back of the van, because from where Mitch and I were standing, we could only see the front of the plain white van, and you could just about make out another man sat in the driver's seat. He was looking down at what I assumed was a newspaper. The second man didn't even acknowledge us, not once lifting his head. I wondered what he was reading because it clearly had him engrossed enough to not care who entered his mobile sweet shop. I would have been nosey and wanting to know everything, but that was me.

Within minutes Kelvin returned with pockets full of goodies and chewing on a Chomp chocolate bar. I wanted one so badly, but I decided to be nice and told Mitch he could go before me.

"Are you sure Von, I don't mind waiting." He smiled.

Mitch had a crush on me and had done for a good while but like I said before, no one in our group knew that John was my new boyfriend. I worried Mitch was only being nice because he wanted to go out with me, so I made sure he went ahead of me. Afterall, I didn't want him to think he'd have a chance of getting with me. *What a mistake that was about to turn out to be.*

"That is the best sweet shop ever." Mitch said with a mouthful of mushed up chocolate and toffee.

"You're only saying that because it is free." I rolled my eyes at Mitch, and he agreed with me. My turn." I said excitedly. I finally knew what the saying meant, "like a kid in a sweetshop," because I was giddy and ran over to the van.

My excitedness was short lived as I got over to the van, for some reason I felt a little on edge the closer I got to the man, which was nothing new for me, being fearful of a fully grown man was normal in my day-to-day life, you would only have to meet my own father to understand. I tried to squash my nerves but something in my gut was screaming at me but I put it back down to knowing I was already defying my father by even entertaining the idea of sweets. With that in mind, I knew I wasn't going to be as greedy as Kelvin or Mitch and I'd have been happy with one sweet treat from the mobile shop. Treats were like a myth to me, and I thought I deserved them after all the chores I'd been doing. Extra chores cause my father decided I needed to learn how to scrub the toilet, which was usually my mother's job, and I didn't feel it was fair to put it on me.

      The man looked down at me and smiled as I climbed up into the back of the transit sized van. He was missing a front tooth, which just made him look sinister. I should have trusted my intuition because something about the man didn't sit right with me, but I placed that thought at the back of my mind, assuming I was feeling on edge just in case my dad found out. Maybe the blokes knew my dad and the van was some sort of test set by him. As doubtful as that may have been, I knew I was breaking one of my father's biggest rules, and I knew the consequences I'd be facing if I were caught. Ignoring my inner voice, I climbed inside. The back of the van was impressive, it actually looked like what I imagined a little shop to be, with shelves full of sweets and boxes of crisps stacked against the back of the van, creating a wall of crisps and other snacks. I decided on a packet of cheesy quavers and a tube of fruit pastels. I grabbed my mouth-watering sweets and was about to lean down to reach for the packet of crisps when I felt the ground move, I stumbled and within a split second the van got darker as the first door slammed shut. I was frozen to the spit, my body in a panic. I maybe should have tried to get out before the other door closed on me, but I was stunned, glued to the spot with my mind racing through thoughts quicker than I could compute. I was hoping it was the wind, hoping it had blown the door closed, but as I tried to stand upright, I felt a hand on me, pushing me down to the floor. The man must have climbed into the van when my back was turned to him.

"What the hell?" I shouted, getting back to my feet and then I heard the engine start up and I knew I was in deep trouble. The van shifted and I feel back down to the floor.

I couldn't see a thing, everywhere was pitch black as boxes of sweets and chocolate bars started to fall in around me. Chocolate bars hurt when they smack you in the middle of the forehead, I can tell you that much. I was scared stiff, literally.

"Let me out!" I snapped before breaking down into tears.

"Shut up little girl." He spoke through gritted teeth.

I remember thinking his accent was weird as he started swearing at the driver to go easier on the corners. He was being thrown around the back of the van, just as much as I was. I managed to move so my back was up against the crisp boxes and stayed quiet as the bloke got very vocal with the driver. I couldn't quite place the man's accent, but I knew he wasn't local. He spoke with broken English so I assumed he was European but where, I couldn't tell you. I was rubbish at geography, it was possibly my worse subject in school. In Wythenshawe you rarely met foreigners, apart from Chelsea Cruise. She was the perfect blonde barbie girl from California and all the boys in our school drooled over her. It was embarrassing.

"And don't you make, sound!" The man hissed at me.

I could tell by the tone of his voice that he wasn't messing with me. I thought my father put the fear of life in me, so I was used to it. The smell of stale tobacco and wet leather coming off the guy just added to the enormity of the predicament I was in. I was seriously kicking myself, I knew the whole thing felt off from the second I saw the van, so why didn't I trust my instincts?

The men clearly knew I was in the van when it started up and the sweet must've been a ploy, to trick kids like me into their van. The man were clever, so I assumed I wasn't their first victim. I did wonder why anyone would want to kidnap me. My parents were poor and the last thing my father would have wanted was any unwanted attention being directed at our family.

How was I going to explain, why I was in the van in the first place?

Maybe I should've been worrying about what was happening in that moment but all that was going through my mind was how much trouble I was going to be in. I knew my father was going to beat me senseless as soon as I got home, regardless of when that would be, I was sure to be later than his curfew.

"Where are you taking me?" I shouted at the man towering over me. My heart was racing, and I felt the fear trying to take over me, but that didn't stop me running my mouth. "My father is so going to kill you." I mocked but I knew full well that my father wouldn't give a shit about me, he'd be more worried about the men who'd kidnapped me.

The man just laughed at me, I couldn't see him properly, I could just about make out his silhouette as my eyes had finally adjusted to the lack of light. He looked taller than he had moments before, a lot taller. Maybe the fear had over exaggerated his size my mind, but he looked like he was built like a brick shit house. Whatever that phrase meant. I'd heard my father use the term plenty of times and always thought it was a weird saying, but it seemed to fit the situation.

"Shut it" The man warned but me being me, I couldn't help myself.

"My father will beat you senseless, I think you need to let me go for your own sake." I said bluffing him.

"I am warning you little girl, shut it, or I will shut it for you."

Something in his voice told me he meant what he said and as much as I didn't want to show my fear, I had zero control over the waterworks that my eyes had created. I had no idea what the men wanted with me and not knowing scared me even more. I was just starting to compose myself when the van came to a sudden stop. My heart was beating out of my chest as I feared we'd arrived at my final destination, but the engine started up again. We must have stopped at a set of traffic lights or junction. I wished I knew my surrounding neighbourhood better as I was attempting to track the movements of the van when it turned each corner. That wasn't too hard to manage when the entire sweetshop moved with the vehicle, but I was quickly losing my bearings through all the turns. My head was going through loads of different scenarios, different ways I could try and get out of the van.

    I felt the vehicle slow down and I pulled myself up to my feet and made a run for the back of the van, trying my hardest to open the doors. I had never tried opening van doors in my life and at the age of thirteen, I'd had no reason to. My feeble attempt failed as the man grabbed me from behind and threw me back down to the floor. He made me whack my head off one of the shelving units and I cried out in pain, I was defeated as I let my body slumped in a heap on the floor.

    It felt like hours had passed as I lay there too scared of being hurt again. I was silenced because the fear of being silenced for good was racing around in the back of my mind. Then the van started to slow down again.

    "Please let me go, please." I begged but he just sniggered at me, then I heard three thuds coming from the front of the van, followed by a male voice shouting at his passenger friend telling him to "Cover the rats' eyes" he meant me.

"Please don't do this." I sobbed.

"Turn around and close your eyes!" I was warned but I did wonder how he'd have known if my eyes were open or not, it was dark in there. My eyes may have adjusted to the lack of light a tiny bit, but it was still pitch black in the back of the van.

"But…" I was about to say when I felt the heat of his hand collide with the side of my cheek. I cried out but more to do with the fear rather than pain. One benefit of having a ridiculously strict father was that my skin could take a good harsh slap from time to time, especially across my face, that was my father's favourite target, because I look like my mother's sister apparently. My father hated the whole of my mother's estranged family. Maybe because they could see straight through him and all of his bullshit.

"You can still make this alright." I said trying to reason with him. "You can let me go, and I won't tell a soul. I promise."

"I will end you little girl." He said through gritted teeth again.

My father would often talk through gritted teeth, so the sound was all too familiar to me, it was my father's way of trying to control his anger, not that he ever did. Control his anger I mean. My father was always heavy handed, but it helped turn me into the tough little cookie I was becoming. Although in that moment I felt anything but tough, I was scared, and knew I couldn't take on two fully grown men.

I was small in height for my age, and actually one of the smallest pupils in my year group at school, but that didn't mean I was a push over. I stopped taking shit from anyone the year previously when I had finally had enough of the bullying at school. I knew the school wouldn't do anything about it, and I also wasn't going to be seen as some grass, telling tales on the bullies because that would have led to so much more shit than anyone needed in school. It didn't help that my father was getting increasingly paranoid and said the bullying would cause too much attention to our family so, I really had no other choice but to stick up for myself and make sure I didn't get bullied again.

I may not have, had the strength to stand up to the bully at home, but the kids my age were easy enough to defend myself against. After all, I needed some sort of victory in my life because I felt like I was on a losing streak with everything else going on around me.

With my losing streak in full swing, it was no surprise I ended up being abducted. It was like fate was definitely not on my side. I was born into a shitty family, I lived in a pretty shit neighbourhood, and I went to a shit, rough school. I basically had a shitty life which I'd never believed could've gotten any worse, but I was gravely mistaken.

***

The van stopped and I was pulled to my feet, then I felt the man's hand on my shoulder directing me to the back of the van. I heard noises coming from just outside as my eyes were covered with some sort of fabric. It remember thinking that the fabric smelled awfully similar to the washing powder my grandmother used to use when I was little, it had a strong lavender scent to it. A stupid thought to go through your head when you're being manhandled I know, but it was weirdly comforting to think she might have been with me, protecting me, maybe. I needed to cling onto any little bit of hope, because I was felt like I was near ready to pass out. Never had I ever feared anything as much as I did in that moment. I didn't know what they wanted with me, and it scared the living daylights out of me.

    I felt the man grabbing me around my waist, trapping my arms against my own body, then he lifted me off my feet. I must have been heavier than he expected because he lowered again to readjust before pulling me back up even higher. He was hurting me, so I kicked out, wriggled, and tried with all my might to break free, but it was no use, he was a lot stronger than me. Within a few minutes, I allowed myself to be defeated, realising I was only wearing myself in the process. Whatever was about to happen to me, I accepted it in that moment and felt a weird air of calm around me. I wanted to believe more than anything that it was my Granny's spirit protecting me. I could see sunlight penetrating through the fabric as soon as that thought entered my mind, so that was my heavenly sign.

    Bright yellows and greens lit up the inside of my blindfold and I could feel the breeze against my calves. Embarrassingly that morning's choice of trousers didn't quite fit me, and I had to convince the lads that it was a new fashion trend about to take off. Three quartered trousers I called them, but in reality, they were aged nine to ten kids jeans, my younger siblings clothes to be exact. I was just fortunate to be skinny enough to fit in them. The washing machine rarely went on at home and it was my chore to handwash all the smaller items like underwear and socks, which we always had plenty of, thanks to me.

    I was placed on the ground and order to walk freely, because I was heavier than expected. I felt myself being shoved forwards every now and again. Then I heard more voices, which made me fearful again, there were more than just two men, it sounded like a whole group of them. *What did they want with me?* I was scared I was about to be gangraped or something and that fear kept me conforming to their demands. I wanted to survive but knew I was no match for a fully grown man, never mind a whole group of them. I thought about trying to lash out again, but then what? I knew I couldn't outrun the men either and I had no idea where I'd been taken to. I could tell we were outside, but we could have been anywhere in Manchester, although Wythenshawe wasn't known for its greenery, which made me assume we had travelled out into the countryside somewhere. I still needed to try, and I pulled my hands up to removed my blindfold, but the bloke behind me noticed and he grabbed hold of me again, lifting me off the ground. I wriggled and squirmed but it was no use, and I felt a sharp blow to the bottom of my back. His elbow I guessed, whatever it was, it was bony and hurt.

"Let me go!" I screamed but my mouth and nose were quickly covered by what I presume was the man's hand. He had a large, manly hand that covered the majority of my face, making it hard to breath.

"Shut her the fuck up, before I silence her for good."

It was a third males voice I heard, he had either a Scottish or Irish accent, I couldn't quite tell. I had distant family members from both sides, and they all sounded the same to me. The words 'silence her for good' repeated in my mind. The pain from being struck, felt like I was bleeding inside my body. Fear washed over me as I thought I was about to die, staying silent was my only option and I knew it.

The light around me started to get a little denser as different shades of greens illuminated through the tiny holes in the fabric. I was convinced we were in the woods. I could smell the mud and the trees. It's funny; being without sight made me realise just how good my other senses were and there was no mistaking the sound of the trees rustling above us. I listened carefully hoping to find a clue in the noises but all I could hear was the birds above us, chipping their little song as if everything was okay in the world. I envied them, life would be so easy if we could just fly away.

After about five minutes of being carried, I was lowered to the floor again and told to hold still. Fear made me conform as I listened in on the men talking between themselves. I counted four male voices altogether and the thought of trying to make a run for it again entered my head, but I was scared stiff and knew deep down that I was fighting a losing battle. I was outnumbered and all I could do was nod my head in agreement, I couldn't even find the strength to speak.

The fabric was rubbing on my nose, making me feel like I needed to sneeze, but I held it in as I was warned not to move a muscle.

"Don't make a single move little one, or he will get rid of you." He said taking hold of my wrist and pulled me back up to my feet.

I needed to know what they wanted with me, what were they were planning to do to me? I didn't want to speak to any of them and I was scared of their response. What if I was taken to the woods to be harmed or even worse, murdered? Knowing that bit of information wasn't going to make the ordeal any easier to deal with, so I saw little point in even asking.

Next thing I knew, I felt a sharp scratch on the inside of my arm, and I wondered if I'd been bitten by an insect, I was worried it may have been a poisonous bug or something as my legs became weak and buckled from underneath me. I fell, landing in a heap on the floor and then everything started to get darker.

CHAPTER TWO – Dark desperation

I was confused as I opened my eyes and almost forgot I'd been kidnapped but then I remembered everything. I was blinded by the bright lights above me and my first thought was, I must be dead. Unfortunately, I wasn't lucky enough to be dead, as I saw the concrete ceiling above me come into focus. My eyes stung from the bare strip light, and I felt groggy and sick to my stomach. My body ached all over like I'd been in a fight with Mick Tyson.

"She's awake." A heard a girls voice and I blinked a few times, as my eyes struggled to focus on everything, the difference in light was really affecting me.

When I managed to open my eyes properly, I turned onto my side, which had me winching in pain. I was shocked to see I was being held in a large concrete room, but I wasn't alone. The men who abducted me were nowhere to be seen and instead they were replaced by two other girls both similar to me in age. I looked down at myself and I was confused to see my clothes had been removed. Just like the other two girls, I had been placed in what looked like a white cotton nightdress from the 1950's, complete with an ugly frilly collar and oversized bow. I wondered if I'd be messed about with while unconscious but that thought made me recoil inside and I guessed I would have noticed if I'd been abused in that way.

"What the actual fuck?" I said out load when I felt something cold against my leg. I looked down to reveal I was handcuffed to a metal pipe running the length of the concrete room. It was a heating pipe, but with the chill in the air, I wondered if the heating was ever on. Both of the other girls were also chained into place, and it confirmed my suspicions, that I wasn't the first girl those two man had abducted.

The room itself was no bigger than a large garden shed. It had no windows and one steel door at the far end. It was literally a grubby, damp concrete square with a strip light above us and an air vent above my head, which was our only source of air, and I couldn't say it was fresh air either. The place smelt damp and dirty, and it held some resemblance of the gross toilets at my school. The boys toilets more like, as the strong stench of urine made its way straight up my nose, turning my stomach inside out.

On my side of the room was a bucket and washcloth and the other side a bigger bucket which I assumed was how we'd relieve ourselves when we needed the bathroom. Underneath me was an old stained, itchy blanket and the thinnest pillow I'd ever seen. My Granny owed thicker pillowcases than what they had us sleeping on. The pillowcase itself wasn't even on the actual pillow, but beside me folded neatly and mine looked like it had blood stains all over it. *Gross.*

"Are you okay?" One of the girls asked and I just wanted to laugh at her.

I knew it wasn't her fault, as humans we ask some stupid shit when we don't know what to say, and what would you say to a young girl who had been just ripped from everything she knew, and caged like an animal, all in the space of a few hours? I didn't answer the blonde-haired girl, my eyeroll was enough of a clue, that I was far from okay.

I remember my head feeling really sore, worse than any headache I had felt in the past and I was shocked when I placed my hand on the back of it, and could feel the dried in blood embedded into my hair. That bloke must have hit me with some force, and I guessed that was why I'd passed out.

I looked over at the other two girls in disbelief and just looked down at the floor. After a few minutes of wallowing in my own self-pity, I finally decided I needed some answers.

"Where are we?" I asked but my voice was hoarse and cracked as the words struggled to leave my lips. I needed a drink, desperately.

"I wish I could tell you." The darker haired girl spoke at first. "We have been here for days and don't even know what they want with us."

"I offered them money, told them my dad has plenty of cash in the bank, but they don't seem to want money." The blonde girl explained.

"They are sick fucks, whatever they want with us, it can't be nice." Piped up the darker haired girl.

"Don't say that Jenny."

"Why? It's fucking true." She snapped back.

I sat and listened in as the two girls started bickering among themselves, the blonde-haired girl wasn't backing down, she told the other girl to calm down and stop guessing because neither of them knew what was going on, the dark-haired girl was called Jenny.

"It doesn't make any sense." She said, "none of it. We are three different people. Leanne here is a little rich kid, whereas my mother's on benefits so it isn't about money or status, and well, we don't know about you." Jenny said and I swear I saw her smirk.

"We're not that rich!" The other girl muttered under her breath.

"Yeah. Right!"

Intrigued, I started asking them both questions, trying to figure out if we did had anything at all in common, but our gender seemed to be the only common ground we shared. I found out Leanne was taken on her way home from choir practice, she would normally be collected by her mother, but that fateful day, her mum was running late, and she may have had the voice of an angel, but she didn't have the patience of a saint, that was apparent. Leanne started walking home and was taken when she walked down an ally way on her own. She had been chained up for four days.

    I assumed it was still Saturday, until that point I loved Saturdays the most as that was the only day I was allowed out, weekdays I would be for school and studying, and Sundays were for housework and meaningless tasks set by my father. He would often remind me that my education was the most important aspect of my life, and I wasn't allowed to have distractions during the week. Being allowed out of the house on a Saturday was only permitted if I'd had all my chores and had all my homework completed. My father would sometimes add on an extra hour onto my homework schedule because he believed the education system was going downhill since he'd finished school thirty years previously. He told me I would thank him when I got older, but I couldn't ever see me thanking that man for anything.

    "I used to love Saturdays." I muttered.

    "It's Monday morning." Jenny explained. "You were out of it for the entire day yesterday."

    "Wow! They must've hit me pretty hard to knock me out." I wasn't really surprised with how sore my head was.

"They probably drugged you; they did with me." Leanne explained.

No wonder I felt in such a daze, I'd assumed I was suffering with a concussion but being drugged made more sense. At first, I thought I'd been bitten by something as I remembered the scratchy feeling just before I'd passed out, but maybe I was injected instead. I wasn't sure how long a concussion was meant to last, but I believed it was measured in hours, and not days.

The realisation had me feeling automatically ill as my stomach tightened and the bile started to rise up my throat, filling my mouth with an acidic liquid and before I knew it, I was over on my hands and knees throwing up all over the floor.

My body ached and I started to shake uncontrollably. I had never been good at being ill, throwing up made me cry most of the time, but I didn't want to cry, not in front of the other two girls. I held back the tears, but my stomach tightened again as a wretched even further.

Jenny and Leanne both looked over at me, both with a look of horror in their eyes. You would've thought I'd just committed the worst of crimes by the looks on their faces. Leanne then explained that the last time she was sick all over the floor, she was forced to eat it, and when she refused, she was beaten into submission. The poor girl was covered in bruises all over her legs and arms, some were recent as they were still reddish in colour, while others were starting to turn a purplish, yellow.

"Clean that up if I were you." Jenny muttered under her breath.

"What with?" I asked.

"How the fuck would I know." Jenny's voice held venom as she looked at me like I was a piece of shit. She was lucky I was chained into place, because I would have normally slapped any girl who thought they could talk to me like crap. Outside that room, we'd have been fighting and even if I thought she'd wipe the floor with me, I refused to take shit from anyone apart from my father.

"Sorry, I shouldn't have snapped." Jenny apologised. "I've just had enough; I wish they would kill us and be done with it."

"Speak for yourself." I muttered, the last thing I wanted to do, was die! As much as my life was rubbish, I had to admit I'd been looking forward to becoming an adult and living by my own rules, although it looked like that was no longer guaranteed. I vowed to myself, that I'd do everything in my power to stay alive, I was too young to die.

"What the fuck do they want with us?" I was trying to hold back the tears falling from my eyes, but it was no use. I was terrified.

"There was another girl here when they first brought me here." Leanne explained. "I guessed she'd been here a while by the looks of her. She didn't tell me much, but she did let slip that it was a woman who runs this place. She told me they are planning on torturing and trafficking us girls."

"How can they get away with this?" I asked but I didn't get a response.

"We are being sold I think." Leanne looked at Jenny before looking back at me. "We don't know for sure, but it sounded like that was what the girl was trying to tell us."

"Where is she now?" I asked but neither Jenny, nor Leanne knew.

"Sold maybe."

"Or maybe not, they said they were getting rid of her." Jenny said and I looked at her in horror.

"So, she could be dead!" Leanne muttered.

The enormity of the whole situation was really starting to sink in. This wasn't just a quick grab of a girl in the heat of the moment, this was a well thought out plan. Those people knew what they were doing, and I suspected they had been abducting girls for a while. I didn't ignore the comment about it being ran by a woman either, what woman in her right mind would abduct and abuse young, helpless girls? She would have to be pretty twisted, that was for sure.

I scanned my eyes around the concrete room again just to see if I could notice any signs of people being here before us, but I was cuffed to a metal pole and I was immobilised, unable to move any further than the stinking buckets. Regardless of being stuck to the spot I still noticed a metal ring, behind where Jenny was sitting.

"Is that a pair of broken handcuffs?" I asked.

Jenny didn't even turn around to look at the metal device that I was talking about, I guessed she'd already seen them plenty of times before. Jenny told both me and Leanne to expect the worst and it wouldn't matter how much we tried to get out of the handcuffs; it was no use. She knew first hand as she'd already tried everything to escape.

"I have tried enough times to get free. I even almost broke my own wrist just to get them off me."

I had no doubt in my mind that Jenny would have tried everything as well, she seemed like a ballsy type of girl. I've may have only spoken to her for a matter of minutes, but Jenny came across as a very streetwise person, whereas little Leanne, not so much. If anyone was going to help us escape, it was going to be Jenny so with that in mind I decided I needed to try and keep her on my side.

***

I'm not sure how long I had been awake, but my throat was really dry and the smell of the sick beside me turned my stomach yet again. It took so much inner strength to stop myself from throwing up again. Time was weird in that cell.

The three of us girls were talking among ourselves when I heard the distinct sounds of a door opening, it must have be an outer door that opened because I couldn't see any movement from the entrance. It was the sound of a metal lock sliding open, followed by a clink of metal and another sliding sound. I then heard a metal hinge swing open and it off the door. My eyes were fixated on the entrance, hoping to catch a glimpse of at least one of the men who'd abducted us, but nothing happened. The room fell eerily silent as all three of us held onto our breaths.

A few seconds later I heard three knocks on our door which I had already been informed by Leanne, meant they were planning to come into the room. One of the men shouted through to us, telling us to cover our faces. So, I lifted my hands up to cover my face, thankfully Jenny whispered to me to use the pillowcase, The beige-coloured cotton pillowcase wasn't for my pillow after all, but to cover my head. I lifted the fabric from the floor, remembering what Leanne had told me about making a mess, and fear washed over me like a tidal wave. It took every ounce of my being not to burst into floods of tears. The other two girl's weren't crying, and I didn't want to appear as weak as I truly felt.

"Hurry up and put it on." Jenny warned. "If they see us looking at them, they will get rid of us. Just like they did with the other girls before us."

Both Jenny and Leanne covered their faces with their own pillowcases, and I did the same.

"Ready!" A males voice echoed through the door.

"Yes, we are." Jenny replied.

I heard a lot of footsteps and assumed it must have been the vile men who'd abducted us. I was scared they were about to take me away to be tortured but didn't dare to show it. I finally released the air I had been holding onto and I could sense someone standing right beside me. I could almost feel the heat radiating from their body and heard something being placed on the floor to the righthand side of me. The same sounds came from where both Jenny and Leanne were sat. Then I felt a tug on my ankle as the handcuff shackling me to the spot, was shaken. The rattling of the metal rang in my ears, and I presumed it was done to make sure I hadn't tampered with it. Heavier footsteps made their way towards me, and then a lighter set of footsteps. I was certain the woman who ran the place was in there with us. I could smell her perfume and then my suspicions were justified as I heard her coughing. It was an unmistakable cough from a woman. I still couldn't wrap my head around the idea that a woman could be involved in any of it, but he presence confirmed it, she sickened me. I hoped to never meet the woman but here she was, in the prison cell with us. I was told by Leanne, that if we were taken to see the psychotic doctor, we might never return, so her presence scared me.

"No funny business." A male voice warns "And who made that mess?"

I stayed silent, scared to speak, scared of being noticed. He clearly meant the yellow bile I'd thrown up just moments before and it was obvious it had come from me as Leanne and Jenny were both too far away from me, to be the culprits. I was half expecting to be struck by one of the men and I braced my body, ready to receive a punch or kick.

Then I was taken back when I heard Leanne as she cried out in pain. I couldn't see what had happened, but it sounded like she had been winded.

Did he just kick her? I was sure I was in for it next.

I'd had my fair share of digs to the stomach to know the sound of being winded, and it was not a nice feeling. My father was the first person to ever wind me back when I was about ten years old. I had felt very brave, encased in my own youthful stupidity, and I purposely defied one of his ridiculous demands. Fair to say I didn't do it again in a hurry as I was rewarded with an almighty punch to the stomach. I felt the effects for weeks and worried he'd broken my ribs or something, but his punishment worked, because I never did question his stupid rules after that day. Well not to his face anyway. Having a father hit you all the time was something I perceived as a normal upbringing, it wasn't until I'd started secondary school, when I realised just how strict my upbringing truly was in comparison to my peers.

In that moment I felt sorry for Leanne but there wasn't much I could have done for her. The footsteps started to move away from us, it sounded like they were leaving the room again.

"Make sure they are well fed and watered, and I will take samples tomorrow morning." The female voice spoke, she sounded European or something.

"Yes mam." A male voice responded, moments later the door slammed closed.

I wanted to take the pillowcase off my face as I was feeling ridiculously hot and faint, I had never been good with confined spaces, but I was too worried that someone was still in the room with us, so I stayed as still as I could. The second door closed, before I heard the locks being slid shut again.

"Samples?" Jenny said as I removed the bloodstained fabric from my head. Thankful for a breath of air, even if it wasn't all that fresh.

"Does she want me to shit in a cup, or summit?" I asked sarcastically.

I know it maybe wasn't the best time to try and joke but if I'd really let myself think about how serious the whole situation was, I would have been no help to anyone. Leanne smiled at me, but I saw the tears in her eyes, and it upset me knowing how trapped the three of us were. There was no way on this earth, we would have escaped through the various doors, even if we were at full strength, we were three teenage girls who were no match for a group of fully grown men, Jenny and Leanne knew that as much as I did, and the three of us looked at each other, feeling helpless.

"Did someone hit you while our faces were covered?" I asked Leanne.

"He kicks her every time he comes in here." Jenny explained. "She took a bite out of his arm when he grabbed her, so it's his little sick bit of revenge on her."

"I swear he swings harder each time." Leanne looked down at the floor. "I hate him, and I don't even know what he looks like."

"My dad used to boot me in the stomach too, the trick is to try and remain relaxed, which I know sounds stupid, but when we tense up our bodies, everything hurts that little bit more." I explained.
"How can a dad do that to his kid?" she asked.

"Beats me. Literally."

I could feel the girls pain as she tried to talk, and it was heart breaking to see. At first I wondered if it was my fault Leanne got the harsh treatment because I didn't clean up the sick on time, one of the men cleaned it up while our heads were covered.

"I think we are getting weaker." Jenny sighed, a long-drawn-out sign as she slumped herself against the wall. "Eat up, otherwise the rats will be in here again."

"Rats!!" I gasped. My skin crawled at the thought.

I looked beside me and saw a cheese sandwich and an already peeled banana. Not the worst food in the world I thought to myself as I picked up the wooden tray from beside me. I was half expecting to find bugs inside my sandwich or somethings else just as horrifying, but it looked safe enough to eat, and Jenny had already eaten half of hers, so I took a bite.
My body hadn't consumed food in two days and just trying to chew what was in my mouth had me wanting to throw up again. I was grateful for the cup of water and drank nearly all of it in one go, before trying another bite of my sandwich which tasted amazing the second time around, considering it was just cheese, butter, and bread, it was well needed.

"Don't rush it, it won't get refilled till late tonight." Leanne said winching as she leant forward to retrieve her own tray.

I didn't care if it was empty, my body needed water more than anything and I drank the contents of the plastic cup and munched the last of my sandwich in two mouthfuls. I had known hunger before, back when I was ten years old, my father forbid me from food for three days, because he caught me trying to steal one of his biscuits. I was ten and wanted so badly to try one of his treats and I had been on my best behaviour, but it wasn't good enough for my father, nothing ever was. I was caught red handed by my younger brother who went running straight to my father and told on me. Thomas was rewarded with one of his biscuits while I was on a food ban.

I was hungry but I also felt nauseated and ready for a sleep. I was knackered. With that being said, I had so much I wanted to know, I needed to know more about the girl before us, intrigued to know what had happened to her.

Jenny started talking about the girl, but something seemed off to me, she said at first the girl hadn't spoken much, but then Jenny was there telling me about her family, and how the girl had become a friend to Jenny. For a girl who apparently didn't speak, Jenny knew a lot of details about her. I got a feeling I wasn't being told the whole story; I just knew she was lying to the both of us, although I couldn't prove it.

Leanne seemed to believe every word Jenny had said and yes maybe I was just being a little paranoid, but could you blame me? I was being held captive in a concrete box! Maybe had I been a little more paranoid before my greed took over, then I might not have been abducted in the first place.

"Jenny you must know something, anything." I felt like I was begging her, and I was.

"Look all I know is she got sick, like really sick and doctor dick lover had her sent away. She said and I quote 'Get rid of her, she is no good to us sick. I never saw Alison after that." Jenny threw her sandwich to the floor. "I tried to get sick myself, to find out what had happened."

Alison! So, much for Jenny not knowing the girls name! I bit my tongue and decided not to pull her up on it, instead I stayed quiet. It proved to me that Jenny wasn't to be trusted. Not that I trusted very easily anyway.

Why would she lie to us, what else was Jenny hiding?

"I am glad you didn't get sick." Leanne said concerningly. "I need you."

"No, you don't kid, you need to get out of here. Maybe being sold isn't all bad." Jenny joked and I couldn't help but grin at her and of course she noticed.

"How can you even joke about it?" Leanne was a little more sensitive and turned her back on Jenny.

I remember thinking it was a little childish, and that led to me ask both of their ages.

"I'm fourteen, Leanne is eleven." Jenny said.

I gasped; shit she really was only a baby. I may have only been a couple of years older, but I had no choice but to grow up sooner than most kids my age. I had always had a good head on my shoulders, even as a small child.
I started to go out of my mind trying to produce a way I could outsmart those people, whatever they were planning to do to us, I decided in that moment I would do everything in my power to stop them. I wasn't willing to go down without a fight.

CHAPTER THREE – Entrapment 101

They must have had set times that they came into us. When I say they, I mean the guards and that stupid posh bitch which we all called the psycho doctor. We were fed twice a day. The food was easy stuff like soups or sandwiches and most of the time we had fresh fruit that had been peeled and chopped before being given to us. The bread thankfully was always fresh which made me wonder whether or not they had another building close by to prepare our food.

I had worked out that it took the female doctor thirteen steps to get over to where I was at the far end of the concrete cell where we were being held captive, chained into place. Why I counted their steps, I didn't know but I felt it was information I may have needed in the future. The room was no more than eighteen foot squared, it took her another three steps between the heavy metal door and the outer door. I calculated the outer door couldn't have been more than 5 feet away. The footsteps sounded muffled but also contained I assumed there was a corridor between the two doors. What was beyond that outer door, I didn't know, but I was keen to find out. None of my calculations were going to be of any use to me if I couldn't escape. I knew I had to at least try something.

Later that evening, the guard's entered our cell to clean up, Leanne had told me that they came in and cleaned the cell, every few days to empty the buckets and wipe down our yoga mats, the thin mat was used as a mattress, but we may as well been on the bare floor as they didn't provide any comfort. As soon as the men left our cell, I noticed one of them had left muddy footprints. The ground outside must have been damp for the soil to attach itself to his boot. I already guessed we were in the woods so it wasn't much help but the footprint itself must have been a size ten to eleven. I only knew that because my father's shoe size was similar.

That had me thinking about my parents and I wondered if they were even looking for me. *Did they even miss me?* My mother would not have done anything without my father's permission, and he would have got ape shit at having any attention directed towards his door. I wondered if he ever cared about me and I knew he'd turn everything on me, somehow I'd be punished, so was I really in any worse of a situation. I wasn't sure, although it was my mother who I felt sorry for the most, I knew she would've been getting the brunt of my father's temper because I was no longer there to be his verbal punching bag.

He better not have laid one finger on her! I could feel my blood reaching boiling point as my thoughts started to take over and for a split second I almost forgot where I was. Pity that naivety didn't last long.

***

    Leanne had been crying off and on all afternoon, but to be fair, we'd had a bit of an ordeal that morning when two of the guards took Jenny off somewhere. Leanne was worried we wouldn't see her again, but I wasn't so sure. I knew Jenny was in the same boat as both Leanne and I, but something about her made me not trust her. Why did the guards take her, and not the both of us as well? Leanne told me I was being paranoid when I voiced my concerns, but she didn't see the way Jenny had been acting. Living with my father, meant I learnt how to protect myself pretty well by reading the signs, I learnt how to read someone, and Jenny was still a mystery to me, that was why I didn't trust her.
    Jenny returned a few hours later but she refused to talk to either me or Leanne and just claimed to be knackered and in need of sleep. I felt that was selfish because I had the right to know what the sick twats wanted with us and unfortunately for us, Jenny was the only one that had left our cell. She must've seen something; she was the only person to see what was beyond our cell, but she refused to say anything. I voiced my concerns and told her she had no right keeping it from us, but she ignored me. Luckily for her I was shackled into place because I wanted to wipe the smug look off her face. I was upset because Jenny knew Leanne and I were both next and she could've given us a heads up, but instead she stayed quiet. I

didn't like Jenny and it became apparent the feelings were mutual.

***

      It was the early hours of that same morning when we had been woken up early. Either I had slept through the warning knocks, or the guards didn't give us time to cover our faces. I was in a state of sleepy shock, and I remembered being lifted to my feet. I heard a few grunts from the guard manhandling me, but I was still half asleep and didn't really understand what he was saying. It was all a bit of a daze and before I finally realised what was happening, there were five guards in the tiny cell with us, ordering us about. I thought it was strange that our faces weren't covered up, but we couldn't really see the guards anyway as they all wore plain black security uniforms, and their faces were covered up with bandanas or ski masks.

      I was pulled to my feet while they covered my head with the pillowcase, and I was pushed and shoved into the thin corridor. We were made to walk for a few minutes before being ordered to sit on the floor and wait. A few minutes later, we were separated, it sounded like Jenny was dragged into another room, maybe next door while both Leanne and I were ordered to stay still. The floor was cold and as I ran my fingertips against it, it felt smooth, like marble. Nothing in comparison to the rough concrete floor of our cell. The room they'd taken us to, was very well lit, I knew that, because the light had penetrated through the thin cotton pillowcase that was covering my face.

"Bring me the first girl." I heard the foreign woman speak. "Strap her to the bed."

I didn't know if she was referring to me, or Leanne until I heard Leanne scream out. I heard cries and grunts, and it sounded like they were beating her, as she fought and begged for them leave her alone. Leanne was pissed off and verbally assaulted the guards when the woman shouted and silenced the room.

"Hold her down, for Christ sake."

Leanne cried a little, that cry turned into a whimper and then she went deadly silent. I had no idea what had just happened, but I suspected the worst. I panicked thinking they'd just killed her, and I wasn't about to let them do the same to me. I may have been blindfolded but I was no longer chained into place and decided to remove my pillowcase, and make a run for it. As I took off the face covering, I saw a small dark-haired woman in a lab coat, with black framed glasses and wearing a black facemask, she was sat behind a white wooden desk too busy looking at Leanne. She didn't look the way I expected, and that threw me of guard a little. I expected a big manly woman, not a little petite thing. I was in the room with three guards, one stood by the doorway, and the other two were stood beside the doctor. All of them were wearing balaclavas or ski masks. The room was white and bright and resembled a nurse's office. No one was looking in my direction so I turned on my heels and darted towards the door, as fast as my little legs could take me.

    "Get her, you incompetent fool!" The woman bellowed just as I got to the door.

    I should've known the door would be locked; Within seconds I was pinned to the floor by the guard closest to me. I kicked and punched, and tried my hardest to break free, but I received a blow to the head that must've knocked me unconscious.
    By the time I came back around I was back in the cell, with both Jenny and Leanne. I quickly realised my arm was sore to the touch. I had either had my blood taken or been injected with something. I assumed the latter option because I had been feeling sick. That sickness lasted for days on end.

***

    We soon found ourselves falling into a routine, our mealtimes were at midday and then again at six in the evening. Even the times we were told to sleep, and woken were on a timetable. Our routine included two trips a week to see the doctor, so she could do weird tests on us. Some days it was just our blood pressures checked and being attached to a heart monitor for an hour, other days, samples were taken from us, that included tissue samples. The messed-up doctor enjoyed slicing parts of our bodies, in places which were tender but harder to see when we had our frilly nightgowns on. I had no idea why we were having samples taken, and I wasn't sure I even wanted to know because every scenario in my head was just as horrific as the one before, so the best thing I could do was try and block it all out.

Blocking things out became easy for me growing up and there were some advantages of having a rubbish family. I had a high pain threshold thanks to my father. From such an early age, I'd taught myself to switch off to the pain and discomfort from the countless run ins with my dad, so my situation didn't feel much different to being grounded at home. Admittedly my father wouldn't have drugged me up or started slicing at me, but the fear I was feeling was very much the same.

I knew that the easiest way for me to get through the doctor's visits, was to remain on my best behaviour, and I think the woman was starting to take a shine to me, mainly because I didn't give her many reasons to hate me, I always done as I was told, unlike Leanne or Jenny. Don't get me wrong, I still feared going to 'The Doctors Office' just as much as the next girl, but I felt like I had some sort of control over it all. I didn't but I convinced myself otherwise because it was easier to deal with.

I was starting to understand why we were there too; Leanne was right when she assumed we were being sold, we were but not until the doctor was one hundred percent happy that we were at full health and the right weight and height for their buyers. Jenny needed to lose a few pounds, so she was put on a food ban for a week. She wasn't starved, but she was given a mushy porridge milkshake instead of sandwiches and fruit. She complained every day for the entire week, but that made me laugh inside, because it was obvious the girl couldn't stand me, and I wasn't particularly fond of her either. The feeling was very much mutual.

As much as I wanted to believe I was coping with my situation well, the stress of it all was starting to affect me, I had been feeling ill for weeks and I wasn't getting any better. I tried to keep it from everyone the first day or so, but then I started actually being sick, and it wasn't so easy to hide. I feared that the doctor would find out and get rid of me. When one of the guards caught me throwing up in the bucket, he warned me to get better soon, because The Doc, couldn't sell me if I was ill. He didn't say she'd be rid of me, so that eased my worries a little.

I was starting to think the young Scottish guard also had a soft spot for me because he seemed kind and would talk softly to me. The man often reassured me that if I done as I was told, no unnecessary harm would come to me. For some reason I felt like I might have been able to trust the guy. After all, he seemed nothing like the rest of the people working in that hellhole. I wondered what would make him ever want to work in a sick place like that, but I assumed they were all scared stiff of the woman in charge of the messed-up organisation.

The Scottish guard I'd nicknamed Seamus because it was the only Scottish name I knew; he didn't seem to mind his nickname. He refused to tell me his real name, no matter how many times I'd asked so a nickname was needed.

Seamus was kind and I couldn't understand how he ended up working in a horrific place like that, again he wouldn't tell me how he ended up there, just that it wasn't that easy to resign. He told me it wasn't the type of job he could've just walked away from and part of me started to feel sorry for him. Seamus made working there sound like a prison sentence. *Was he just as trapped as me?*

The other guards hated me, and they made that abundantly clear. The one guard who really stood out was the big dude, he looked like a bouncer and was the person who rugby tackled me to the floor when I tried to make a run for it. He wasn't the nicest of blokes, and talked to us girls like crap and muttering under his breath at us, Leanne said she thought he was German. He spoke broken English. I wondered if he was related to the doctor in some way, but I never did find out. Leanne and I nicknamed him "Hans," and he hated it.

***

Leanne had her back to me, she was sobbing to herself. I tried to console her as much as I could being two meters apart, but my words were pointless, not that it stopped me from trying. The fact that she was so young, really grated on me. Two years difference was all it was between us, but it felt like a decade apart, and I partly felt a responsibility to her.

"You do know she'll be back soon. She always is." I said talking about Jenny who had been AWOL again since early that morning.

Leanne saw Jenny as the mother figure of our group because she was a little older than the both of us and she looked a lot older too. Jenny was one of those teenage girls who were blessed with a mature face and the body of a woman. I, on the other hand had always looked younger for my age and would not have had the luxury of clubbing like Jenny had.

That was where Jenny was abducted, outside the club, waiting on her taxi home. As far as she was concerned, she had got into her booked taxi, after dancing all night with an attractive guy, who was at least five years older. She was on cloud nine but as it turned out, she had just sealed her own fate by getting into the wrong car. Half intoxicated, it wasn't until the taxi stopped in a dark side street that Jenny realised, she was in danger. After a struggle she eventually went limp as the coliform took effect. Jenny woke up chained to the wall. Six weeks she'd been chained to that wall before I got there, and I was starting to lose count of how many days I'd been captured.

"She has been gone all morning." Leanne sobbed, "she is never gone this long."

"This is Jenny we are talking about; she'll be fine." I said the words but something in my gut, told me I was mistaken.

"What if she has been sold?" Leanne said, still sobbing to herself.

"Then lucky her, it has to be better than being stuck here." I said, and I started to wonder what being sold would actually be like.

"What if she's been sold to have sex with men?" Leanne sounded horrified by her own words.

"I didn't think about that," I said, and I hadn't. My mind could get very dark, but that thought made me feel ill. "or we are being sold to some rich family to become their live-in maid." I preferred my option to Leanne's, being a cleaner didn't sound so bad.

Jenny was gone for the majority of the day. When she finally returned, she didn't say much. She just told us that she didn't want to talk about it and that she was asked a lot of questions. She did not tell us the whole story, but I planned to get it out of her and felt like we had a right to know what we were about to endure. She didn't give anything away though, and the more I pushed her, the moodier she became. Jenny hated that I always questioned her, and it caused a divided between the three of us.

***

The Scottish guard was usually the one who would bring us in our food and that day I had been feeling sicker than usual. I was suffering with hunger pains like I desperately needed to eat. The three knocks on the door couldn't have come at a better time as my stomach started to rumble again, I had never been much of an eater, but I felt starving since I'd been taken. I half expect to see Jenny when we remove our pillowcases, as she was taken again that morning. I hated that she got to leave the cell, and we didn't. It felt unfair. Jenny was taken from our cell within twenty minutes of us been woken up and she didn't return until later that evening, again she refused to talk about what was happening to her and at that point, I knew it was pointless even asking, but I still did, just to be defiant. It was clear that she was hiding something, and I wondered if it was a relationship with one of the guards, but she denied it of course and later in the evening Jenny had tried to turn Leanne against me by saying I was just causing more heartache, but even Leanne was starting to wonder, who Jenny really was, and why she was so secretive. Jenny absolutely hated that I asked her if she was screwing one of the guards and instead threw it back in my face, saying I was the one with the hots for Seamus. She was out of her mind, and I agreed that the Scottish guard had started having more conversations with me, but it was only ever trivial things, like asking how I was feeling or if I had eaten enough. He believed me feeling so ill was down to stress and not eating well. Two things I had zero control over. Having Seamus as an ally was something I wouldn't have expected but I enjoyed the feeling of someone else caring about my wellbeing and I understandably lapped up all of his attention.

  After weeks of reassurance from Seamus, I assumed he was a friend so I started asking him my own questions, hoping to find out something that would help me in some way. I did ask him if Jenny was sleeping with one of the guards, but he told me he had no way of knowing and that if anyone was ever caught fraternising with the prisoners, they would have been dealt with, which usually meant they would be killed off.

  Seamus was taking a massive risk even talking to me and I appreciated him putting himself in harm's way, for me. After all no one else had before then.

***

  Leanne ate her sandwich and lay down; she had been sleeping off and on but every now and again she would wake up screaming. Her poor mind was tormenting her as she thrashed her body about in her sleep. I would hate to have been in her mind, it seemed like a very dark place. I never really dreamt much, and I was thankful of that. The chain that kept her in place rattled against itself as she moved from side to side. It made an eerie sound at the best of times, but on that night it seemed deafening.

I remember feeling frustrated because I obviously couldn't sleep and I was trying to listen in to the faint voices on the other side of the door but with Leanne's nightmarish racket, I couldn't make out a word that was being said. Something was happening and my stomach was in knots as if I were waiting for the shit to hit the fan.

Leanne finally settled again and within minutes the sound of her heavy breathing was making me feel sleepy, I lay my head down and found myself wondering about my family again. I never thought I'd have seen the day I missed being back at home, in my own bed, but I was starting to feel homesick.

***

I was woken to the sound of the metal door being bashed. I looked over at Leanne who was clearly startled and rushing about to find her pillowcase. My heart was in my chest. It was a horrible way to be woken and I doubt anyone could've gotten used to being woken up so abruptly.

"Ready?" A guard shouted through to us, but I didn't recognise his voice.

"Yes." I shouted back.

"Keep them' covered or you'll regret it girls." The guard warned us as the lock on the door started to open.

"Hurry the fuck up, in and out." He said, he was talking to someone else, so I knew he wasn't alone.

"Let me go!" I heard the screams of a girl, and not Jenny either. The monsters had taken someone else!

"Shut up little one, or you'll have the same fate as your little friend here, and you don't want that now do you?" The guard sounded like he was a local man, with his Manchurian accent.
"Please let me go." The new girl sobbed.

"You'll be fine with these girls; they will look after you. Won't you?" He made sure to shout the last two words.

"Yes."

"Yes." Both Leanne and I responded, knowing our punishment if we didn't.

"Put that one over there." I heard the new guard saying.

A scurry of feet echoed over by Leanne, and I assumed they were placing the new girl between us.

I had noticed on the first day of being in that cell that there were seven chains in the room. One of which was broken but it left enough room for six girls to be held in there: Leanne, Jenny, and myself, leaving room for three others.

"Okay, okay, I am moving." I heard Jenny enter the room.

The rattling of the chains echoed in the room as both Jenny and the new girl were chained into place. A few grunts from the guard and the metal door was slammed closed again. We removed our pillowcases.

The new girl started screaming, and threw herself to the floor. Then I saw what had made her so distraught as I gasped in horror at the dead body in the cell with us. The small girl who can't have been any older than nine or ten, still wearing her school uniform. Her body was slumped in the corner of the room with what looked like a bullet hole in the middle of her forehead. Leanne was the next person to notice, and she screamed out in panic. I thought I was very odd that Jenny didn't look; instead, she turned her back to us and faced the wall. There was no point in asking Jenny what had happened, because she never told us anyway, so instead I tried to talk to the new girl, but she was too upset to respond to me.

I had never seen a dead body before and nor had I expected to. The dead girls lips looked almost grey in colour and the hole in her head resembled some Halloween special effect, but I wasn't stupid and knew just how real the whole situation was. The dead girl must have been the new girls friend. How awful.

Was it even real, or was I stuck in a horrific nightmare myself? I wanted more than anything for that moment to be a horrible dream, but I knew deep down that my nightmare had only just begun.

CHAPTER FOUR – Rotting corpse

There was something going on with Jenny, I just knew it. She had hardly spoken a word to any of us since the new girl was captured. I felt like she was feeling guilty about something, but Jenny just got more and more nasty any time Leanne, or I asked any questions. I started to wonder if she was helping the Doctor, maybe running back, and telling the woman what we were talking about. I just knew in my gut that she couldn't be trusted, and I needed to find out why.

The new girl was called Stacey, she was only ten years old and had been abducted from her local park with her friend Alana. Alana put up a good fight and Stacey didn't say much but it sounded like the struggle inevitably got Alana killed. Her dead body was still slumped up against the wall in the far corner, reminding us that it could also be our fate, if we didn't do exactly as we were told. Alana's body was in that room with us for three days straight and her rotting corpse had started to let off a real stink. I had never experienced a smell quite like that, it was almost like rotting chicken or something. Which wasn't helping with my sickness bug at all. I had been throwing up yellow bile for days and I did wonder why I was the only one feeling so bad when the other three all seemed healthy enough.

"Look the other way, I need to pee." Jenny snapped at me, but I was already facing the other way, retching over my own bucket.

"I hate being sick." Stacey said to me sympathetically.

"Me too." Came Leanne's response.

Jenny finished peeing and told us we were allowed to turn back around; I faced Leanne and Stacey purposely. Mainly so Alana wasn't right in my perifocal vision but also because I was in a mood with Jenny who started staring at the rotting corpse, like she was in some sort of weird trance. I think she was hoping for some sympathy, but she wasn't going to get any from me, something about that girl was really starting to grate on me.

"You are punishing yourself, starring at her you know." I pointed out, but Jenny didn't respond to me.

Not that I had expected her to, I was honest and told her I didn't trust her, so, she gave me the silent treatment, which just screamed out guilt to me.

It was a good while of being sat in silence before we heard the three thuds on the door. I placed my pillowcase over my head and heard Leanne prompting Stacey to do the same. Twice a day the guards entered our cell, to bring us food and check on us. Twice a day we had to place those pillowcases over our faces, unless we were visiting the doctor, but Stacey still needed reminding every single time.

    She was too young for all of this, the poor girl was so scared, crying out for her mum most of the time, but while those guards were in with us, she stayed completely silent, just like the rest of us.

    "Ready?"

    Leanne and I responded in unison. Seconds later the doors were open, and I heard the guards standing over in the corner of our cell, next to Alana's body. I hoped to God that they were finally removing her body because I felt like we'd been punished for long enough.

    I was gravely mistaken as I felt a large hand grabbing me from under my arm and pulling me up to my feet. I felt weak and struggled to steady myself as the shackle from my ankle was removed and I was pushed forward indicating that I was to walk with them. More tests and samples were needed and after being in that hell hole for just over a month, I was becoming used to being the Doctor's personal pin cushion.

    Thirteen steps to the metal door, where I was told to wait. The Scottish guard was back off his holiday, which made me feel a little more at ease. I wasn't sure why, but I felt safer with him, than I did with any of the other people in that place.

    Hans on the other hand, scared the living shit out of me. We had no idea what he looked like because everyone's faces were covered at all times, but, in my head, I'd imagined he looked like Arnold

Silent Hope | Sarah Louise Rosmond

Schwarzenegger. Built like a tank and able to swish me in an instant. I managed to get a little glimpse of his eyes the day I'd attempted to escape, but I never saw his face. To be honest, looking at him was the last thing on my mind while he was rugby tackling me to the ground. Hans has ice blue eyes, which sent slivers down your spine.

I was ushered into the small corridor, another four small steps forward and I heard the door to our cell being closed before the door in front of me opened.

All I could hear were footsteps and heavy breathing. The Scottish guard still had hold of my arm, but he'd twisted it behind my back, even though he knew I wasn't stupid enough to try and break free, I think he liked knowing he had the control. I had made that mistake of trying to run for it once before and still had the odd bruise as a reminder.

The outer door was closed, and I was led down a darker hallway, it was a different route to the one I'd have normally taken to the doctor's office, and I worried for my safety, worried I was about to be sold or something far worse.

"Wait here." I was ordered, the grip from my arm loosened and for a second I was stood on my own, no shackles and no one manhandling me.

My freedom didn't last long as Seamus grabbed me by my wrist and pulled me towards him. We entered a well-lit room; the light penetrated through my pillowcase, it was bright and stung at first while my eyes adjusted to the change of light. I felt a breeze against my arm, and it was a welcoming feeling. I knew we weren't outside but assumed I had just passed an open window and it seemed warm outside. Seventeen steps forward before I was directed to my right, and I took another twenty-eight steps forward. Seamus must've sensed I was attempting to track my movements because he told me I was about to be lifted off the ground. I told him it wasn't necessary, but he said he'd been ordered to carry me the rest of the way by the doctor herself. It was as if they knew I was trying to map out my surroundings, and it frustrated no end.

"I am fine to walk." I explained but I was told I had no choice in the matter. "Careful of my stomach please, I have been feeling sick all week."

I regretted saying anything to him as little did I know, it was about to be used against me. A door opened in front of us, and I was lifted up into Seamus's arms. My nightdress was up by my waist, the slight breeze against the top of my legs made me shiver, it wasn't cold but being caged up for ages, had my skin lapping up the fresher air.

"She is feeling unwell ma'am." He said before placing me down on a cold leather chair. I shuddered, like a surge of electricity traveling down the centre of my spine.

"Unwell?" The harsh tone of the crazed doctor echoed throughout the room. I found out through asking questions, that she was Russian. No wonder she was so psychotic, no offence to Russian's but they didn't exactly come across as soft and gentle souls.

I was starting to panic a little, as I still had no idea what she had in store for any of us. Leanne and I believed they wanted to do experiments on us, Jenny reckoned we were going to be sold on the illegal market, either way I knew we were all royally screwed, and just the sound of the doctors' breathing had me on edge.

"I have checked her bloods and there are raised levels of hormone in her body, when did she last bleed?" The crazy Russian doctor asked. "Well..." she snapped and then I realised she was taking to me, not the Seamus.

"I, erm... I," Broken words fell from my mouth.

"I cannot hear her with that stupid thing over her face. Take it off." The woman demanded, "but make sure the little cowards eyes are covered. Here use this."

I heard a few footsteps including her heels on the tiled floor moving away from me. Then I sensed the guards face near to mine. I jumped out of my skin because I wasn't expecting it. I was then pulled back up off the leather chair and made to walk forwards in the direction of the doctors footsteps seconds before.

Seamus whispered in my ear, "do what she has says please, for you own sake. Close your eyes." He released my elbow and told me to stand still.

I felt a little betrayed by Seamus, but I still did as I was told, and I soon felt the pillowcase being lifted from my head. The air touching the skin on my face made all my tiny hairs stand on end, as if it were the first ever time I'd felt a breeze against it. I struggled to stand still, I was unsteady on my feet, and it took every part of my being to resist opening my eyes and trying to get a glimpse of the place I was being held captive, but I was far too scared of what would happen to me if I did.

A few seconds seem like an awfully long time in that situation and eventually a blindfold was placed over my head to cover my eyes. The sensation of being able to breathe normal air again was a shock to me and the air tasted fresh and clean for a change, which just added to the consent reminder of the horrid stench which was occupying our prison cell. A rotten corpse will do that to you, and it was no wonder I was feeling sick all of the time.

"I will ask again and this time I want an answer." She spoke, her voice was very abrupt and demanding.

"I haven't had one." I explained.

"Okay so we have a virgin who hasn't started her menstrual cycle yet, but you have raised hormone levels, why is that?" she asked, but I thought she was meant to be the doctor.

"I am not a virgin." I said quietly, embarrassed, and also scared of how she was about to react.

"Speak up child!"

"I am not a virgin." I stated.

"You are only thirteen years old." She said as if I didn't know my own age.

"Yes, that is correct." I said, but I felt like I was answering the woman back, and that wasn't my intention.

I was just annoyed at the questions and how she was asking me. I may not have been able to see her, but it felt lie she was looking down on me, like I was scum, and she was the only scummy human in that room.
I could hear her mumbling in Russian under her breath while typing ferociously on the keyboard. I felt like I had been standing for ages, my head started to feel light and faint.

"Cover her face up again." The crazy doctor snapped at the guard.

It was obvious I had angered this woman who was now taking her frustration out on the guard trying to put the cover back over my face. I heard something being bashed about, her hand maybe on what sounded like a metal table. My body froze, waiting on her to take that temper out on me, but by the sounds of things, it was Seamus who was getting the brunt of her anger. I could hear him apologising and grunting as she physically started attacking him. I just stood there, unable to see but that didn't stop me from fearing for my life. She was crazy and Seamus was profusely apologising. It sounded as if he was just as scared of the woman, as I was.

Finally, the pillowcase covered my face again and I felt a hand move to my wrist, at first I thought the crazy Doc had taken hold of me, but the hand felt rough to the touch, it was the Seamus. I assumed he was about to take me back to my cell, but instead his grip around my arm tightened even more.

"That hurts." I cried out in pain, but I was ignored by the both of them.

The next thing I knew, I was being lifted up and thrown over his shoulder, he walked a few paces with me. I wiggled to try and break free, but it was no use. His grip was far too strong for me. The next thing I knew, I'd been thrown down on what I assume was a hospital bed. My arms were pinned down either side of my waist and I felt the coldness of leather and metal on my skin. I was being fastened down.

I started to panic, waving my legs about in a hope that I could kick one of them in the face.

"Pin her down and be quick about it, I haven't got all day!"

"Yes Ma'am."

I tried to fight him off, I was thrashing my legs about, trying to kick any part of him possible. I must've knocked off his ski mask off in the process because I felt his beard brush against the heel of my foot. I wasn't sure why, but I'd guessed he was clean shaven up until that point. Now I needed to completely reimagine what he looked like in my mind. Guessing all their appearances was like my little game, something to pass the time, not that I ever believed I would get the chance to see any of their face, but that didn't stop me from feeling gutted that I'd gotten Seamus's appearance so wrong.

"Please, you are hurting me." I screamed out.

If I was being honest, he wasn't hurting me at all, the man was like a gentle giant, but I'd hoped by telling him he was, he might have felt a little sorry for me, but instead he hissed at me to shut up. If I thought he'd betrayed me before, I was mistaken. Seamus was a friend in my eyes, but he was treating me just as bad as the rest of them, and in that moment I hated him, just as much.

Both my arms were secured, and I felt him move to my ankles. My right leg was sore anyway from being chained up for so long, but I gave up wriggling, there really was little point in me trying, and I didn't have any more energy to fight. It was easier to give in, but I wanted more than anything, to see what was happening, because then maybe I wouldn't have been so scared.

I heard a chair slide across the titled floor towards me and the Doctor coughed before she took her seat. It sounded like the guard had been shoved to one side while she muttered that she didn't have the time for me.

I was lay there, fighting back the tears when I heard the sound of a girl screaming, I had heard the girls in my cell screaming and it wasn't coming from them three, so it had to be a new girl. I did wondered if

Jenny, Leanne, and Stacey were next on the doctor's list, or if the punishment I was about to receive was solely for me.

"You can try and be a little more competent, or you'll be out that door in an instant. Do I make myself clear?" The crazy Doc, shouted. She was reprimanding Seamus.

"Yes ma'am, I am sorry."

I was a little surprised to hear how shaky his voice was as he responded to her. There was no denying that she sounded like a scary woman, don't get me wrong. I often wondered what lengths she went to, in order to control these fully grown men. My mother would have told me, I had a vivid imagination, and I would often escape into my own mind as a form of protection.

Before seeing the crazy Doc, I had pictured her pretty because let's face it, she had to be beautiful, how else would she had gotten a load of men to do her bidding, they all wanted to sleep with her. I don't know why; I'd be scared she'd start cutting bits off them as soon as they fell asleep, I reckoned she was a black widow, maybe she devoured her lovers afterwards, I wouldn't have put anything past her. As far as television shows and the rare book had taught me, scientists and doctors were usually stupidly rich, and I assumed the same for our psycho doctor. She had to have some sort of hold over them all, but I couldn't for the life of me, guess what it was. I wasn't sure what the going rate for a teenage girl was, but I'd imagined we weren't all that cheap, maybe they were getting paid shitloads, but Seamus did make me feel like he was just as trapped in the compound and us girls, and maybe he was.

The doctor moved her attention to my wrist, squeezing it tightly. It was obvious she hated me in that moment because I'd just caused her even more work, and she wasn't about to let me live it down. First she placed a band around the top of my arm, pitching my skin, with the elastic, then she wiped the inside of my arm with a damp gauze, it was a cold and wet and made my hairs stand on end, she was taking my blood yet again. I had my bloods taken five times by that point; I was starting to get used to it. That didn't stop me from hissing at her through my teeth as the needle penetrated my skin. I felt her turn her body away from me and she started speaking to someone, but she wasn't speaking a word English, so I tried switched off to her. Then I realised there were more than just the three of us in the room.

All of a sudden, I was feeling lightheaded and thought I was about to throw up. I felt like my eyes were trying to roll to the back of my head and then I realised, she wasn't taking my bloods, she was putting me to sleep.

***

I woke up to the sounds of screaming and I was stunned when to find myself unmasked and without a blindfold, but I wasn't back in my cell. I was unsure where I was, but it resembled a clinical hospital ward. Everything was bright and clean, but I thought I was strange that I was in the ward on my own. The beds either side of me were empty and they didn't look like they'd ever been used.

Was I saved? Did someone find me unconscious? A rush of relieve washed over me and I thought for a second that I was away from that compound and safe. Tears dripped down my cheeks as I tried my hardest to sit myself upright, hoping to see more of my surroundings. The cold reality hit me as soon as I realised I was still strapped down like an animal.

In that moment I knew deep down that I was definitely not out of the woods, instead I was being treated like some messed up, mental patient. *What did they wanted from me?* I lay there crying to myself, wishing it would all end. I found my mind heading towards some dark thoughts as I believed life would be better without me in it, at least I wouldn't be suffering anymore, and it wasn't as if I was going to missed by anyone. The thoughts of taking my own life scared me but I realised I was a coward; I could have never gone through with any of the horrific scenarios in my mind. Feeling defeated I laid my head back down on the soft pillow, thankful for some comfort below me and I closed my eyes, only to be startled by an almighty howling a few minutes later.

It was useless trying to drown out the screams from the other room and I worried that was soon to be my own fate. The tears dripped down each side of my face, making a pool of salty water, nest in the bend of my ear lobe.

"What did I do, to deserve this?" I asked quietly, hoping a higher power would hear my cry for help.

I wasn't a religious girl, but I'd have prayed to the devil in the moment if I believed it would have helped.

The screams continued to get louder until suddenly they just stopped. An eerie silence filled the room around me. *Had they just killed someone else?* That reminded me about the dead girl in the cell, all I could see was Alana's face haunting me. *Why did I let myself think about her?* I assumed her body was still in the cell, rotting away and making any air left in there almost unbearable to breath in. I had no idea how long it took a dead body to start to decompose. It was something I never found myself needing to know but I was curious. Surly it couldn't be healthy, being couped up in the same room as a rotting corpse. It was like something out of a horror movie, not anything you would ever expect to experience in real life. That was exactly what that place felt like, a horror movie. With any luck zombies were about come out of nowhere and eat me alive or better still, a camera crew would appear, and I would find out the whole ordeal was some candid camera setup or something. Wishful thinking, I knew, but I was losing all hope by that point.

The double doors at the far end of the ward made a noise before they swung open. Two females walked into the room, followed by a guard who was pushing someone in a wheelchair. It took me a few seconds before I realised it was Leanne in the chair, sat there, motionless. *Was she still alive?*

I watched on silently, through fear of them coming over to my bed. The nurses were wearing surgical masks which covered the majority of their faces and the guard had on a black ski mask making all three of them hard to identify, which frustrated me. They were clever, and kept themselves covered up.

"Strap her down and then come on, the boss said she needs us urgently." The guard warned the nurse opposite him. None of them took any notice of me, thankfully.

I may not have been able to see their faces, but her body language screamed out fear to me, it was if they were all scared of the boss bitch. I guessed he was referring to was our crazy Russian doctor.

"Oi, what are you doing." I heard a man's voice in the distance. It was faint but sounded like someone was getting a good telling off.

I lay as there as quietly as I could, still not wanting the guard or nurses to notice I was awake, but he turned and walked straight towards my bed. *Shit, I've been seen!* I closed my eyes, sure that I was caught out and fearing what was going to happen once they knew I was awake. I lay there as still as physically possible, my mouth so dry that my lips felt like they were sticking together, and my heartrate was increasing at a rapid speed. I felt the pounding in my head as I held onto my breath. The footsteps got closer to me. And even though I heard him approaching, I still jumped at the sound of his voice.

"Keep an eye on this one too."

He didn't notice my movements, thankfully.

"Yes Sir." One of the nurses replied.

Why were they all so scared? I actually couldn't get my head around the idea that all these people where quite happy to treat young girls they way that they did. *If none of them wanted to work there, then why did they?* I couldn't believe that no one spoke out about us girls and that nobody questioned what was going on, it was like they were all programmed to do as they were instructed.

My mind started wondering off and I decided the doctor must have used some form of mind control, either that, or she had a massive hold over them all. Maybe she was part of a mafia and had threatened to murder their families if word were to ever to get out. It didn't matter what the reasoning was, I didn't understand how women could hurt and abuse young girls, I thought we were meant to have a built-in maternal instinct, but clearly not.

The footsteps stopped, as the guard turned on his heels, I listened on as the three of them made their way back out of the room, with the empty wheelchair in tow. I purposely waited until I heard the double doors swinging closed again before I dared to open my eyes.

I was right, it was Leanne lay in a bed opposite me, she had a drip attached to her arm and she looked pretty frail for an eleven-year-old girl. Her arms and legs were strapped down like mine.

"Psss." I said trying to get her attention, but she didn't respond.

"Leanne." I whispered again but still no response.

I worried that they'd seriously hurt her, and the screams I'd heard just moments before could have belonged to her, although I'd heard Leanne's screams in the past. I didn't to know whether she was dead or alive. I didn't take my eyes off her, waiting for her to wake up or move slightly. I was watching her for what seemed like ages and dozed off a few times in the process. We did a lot of waiting in that hellhole, but we never quite knew what we were waiting for.

Eventually Leanne woke up although very groggy, but she was awake enough to look at me in disbelief. Then it was as if the penny finally dropped, along with Leanne's jaw.

"She said you were dead." Leanne whispered.

"Dead? I am right here. Who said that?"

"Jenny."

"Where is Jenny?" I asked.

"She said they killed you because you're pregnant."

"Oh, did she now? well I wouldn't believe a word that bitch says anyway. Jenny has been hiding things from us, this whole time." I reminded her.

"How do I know you haven't been hiding things Siobhan? You've been gone for days." Leanne sounded annoyed with me.

I knew she liked Jenny, but the girl must have been deaf or blind, because it was obvious, something wasn't right with Miss Jennifer Dawson. Even Leanne admitted that Jenny was caught lying to her face, yet she was sat in the bed opposite me, defending the girl. *Maybe Jenny had managed turn her against me after all.*

I looked over at Leanne stunned. "I don't know where that came from, but it isn't true, as you can see. I had my bloods taken and woke up strapped to this bed. Very much alive."

I was trying to whisper, but I was struggling to contain my emotions. W*hy would Jenny have told her I was dead?* Clearly I wasn't but Leanne still looked over at me like I was a ghost. Jenny telling Leanne I was pregnant was ridiculous and I was even more annoyed at Jenny, than I was before.
That comment got my deep in thought, and I realised that was the reason the doctor had asked me when my last period was. She did mention elevated levels of hormone. *Shit! Surely, I couldn't be pregnant.*

"I am not pregnant Leanne, I can't be." I was trying to convince myself, just as much as Leanne.

"Then why did Jenny hear the guards being told to get rid of you then because they can't sell a pregnant child? You are meant to be dead!"

"I don't know why but there must be some sort of a mistake. As you can see, I am very much alive."

"Maybe Jenny heard wrong, or they just haven't got around to killing you yet."

I looked over at Leanne, stunned that she'd just spoken to me in that way. The Leanne id met just over a month before, wouldn't have spoken the same way, she had a go at Jenny for talking about shit like being killed off, yet she'd just said it to me like it was inevitable. I tried my hardest, but I couldn't hold back the tears. Things honestly couldn't have gotten any worse.

Thirteen years old and pregnant, was this really about to be my life? I touched the side of my stomach with my fingertips, I could reach any further and found myself wondering what it would be like to be a mother, but what was the point in even dreaming about being a mum, if I wasn't going to live long enough to experience it.

What I didn't understand was; if the doctor wanted me taken care of, then why didn't she have me killed off while I was unconscious, she could have easily injected me with something to keep me asleep forever, but instead I woke up in a hospital bed, thinking I'd been given a second chance. Maybe she wanted to keep me to sell the baby. I'd already been in captivity for over six weeks, another seven months wouldn't have made much different to me, as least I would still be alive.

CHAPTER FIVE – What about the baby?

I had been in and out of sleep for days on end and had no idea what time of the day or evening it was, the curtains were drawn closed all of the time, so we could only guess. I was starting to worry because they had been putting crap into our bodies, to keep us lethargic and sleepy, easier to manage us if we're all drugged up but I did worry what effect that was all having on my unborn baby.

    I didn't want to believe that I was pregnant at first and tried to convince myself, it was a mistake, but it was confirmed by Seamus later that day. Seamus was the only person in that hellhole that spoke to me, and with Leanne taking Jenny's side, the Scottish guard became my only ally, well as much as an ally could be to you, in a place like that. I think he felt guilty for betraying me and the man went out of his way daily, just to check up on me and make sure I was okay.

    He said he felt slightly responsible for me, which I thought was a weird thing to say but I put it down to him being involved in the abduction process, he was the driver the day I'd been snatched. *Why didn't he feel responsible for the others?* Regardless of his reasons, Seamus made it abundantly obvious that he had a soft spot for me. *Why else would he take the time to come and speak to me every day?* Even if he only had the time to come and say goodnight to me before the end of his shift, he made sure I knew he was there. I never, once saw him talking to any of the other girls, which made me feel special.

The night Leanne informed me of my condition had turned me into an emotional mess and I was terrified I was going to be killed off, I was scared to my wits end and refused to let myself fall to sleep, even if the drugs they had been pumping into me had other ideas. I honestly thought I was a goner when Seamus abruptly entered the ward. I assumed he was the one tasked with my killing which I thought was fitting, as he did help to abduct me in the first place, but he wasn't there for any reason, other than to check up on me. While stood by the foot of my bed, he confirmed I was about six weeks pregnant. He congratulated me, like it was a reason to celebrate. I couldn't believe it; I didn't want to believe it. Shocked and scared I started to cry, they were silent tears which dripped down both of my cheeks, but Seamus assured me he had a plan that would benefit the both of us.

I laughed at him when he told me he would do everything in his power to keep me safe and I told him what Leanne had said about me being dead. Even though I couldn't see all of his face, his eyes said enough for me to know Leanne was being truthful. Seamus admitted that there were talks about getting rid of me, but he'd managed to get the doctor to change her mind. When I asked how was that possible, he told me to not worry about it. How could I not worry about it, I had a bounty on my head, and I was immobilised and strapped down to a bed, it wasn't as if I had any say in any of it, but it's okay because Seamus said so.

Why was this man helping me? What was he expecting in return?

My head was all over the place and I think he expected me to be grateful or something. He tried to say he'd already saved my life once and that I needed to trust him, but it was him and his groupies who put me in that position in the first place. *How could I have ever trusted him?* and to feel grateful about it too, sounded narcissistic to me. He then had the cheek to tell me I was lucky to still be alive, but I felt anything but lucky.

***

The days that followed saw even more girls being placed in the ward with me, girls of all ages, races, and backgrounds, *how the hell were these monsters getting away with this?* Four new girls altogether. I was half expecting to see Stacey or Jenny, but after three days there was no sign of either of them. Part of me wondered if they had been sold already or whether they were still in the cell with the remains of Alana. Proof that one wrong move could lead to a bullet in the brains.

It was the same two nurses who would bring the girls into the ward, they would wheel them in unconscious and strap them to the beds, some girls came around within minutes, others took a lot longer to wake. It was like a waiting game as I would try to guess the time it would take each girl to wake up. It sounded a little mean, but I had nothing else to do.

It was on the fourth day when the nurses wheeled Stacey into the ward, and they placed her in the bed on the far end of the room.

Every time they filled up another bed, I half expected to see Jenny, but I hadn't seen her since the day they took me from my cell. I had tried to find out more information through Leanne, but she was just as much in the dark as I was. The last time she'd spoken to Jenny was when Leanne had been told I'd been murdered, which still didn't sit right with me. How would Jenny of heard that information in the first place, if she weren't sleeping with one of them? Maybe it was Seamus, I smiled to myself, although I had never seen him talk to any of the other girls apart from me, so it wasn't likely.

I could tell there was something really messed up going on and had I had an ounce of energy, I would have tried and get to the bottom of it, but all the drugs they were pumping into me, had taken every single ounce of energy out of me and any hope of being rescued went along with it.

***

I was woken by one of the nurses, an injection the top of my arm. I felt myself drifting in and out of sleep. I had already been in and out of sleep for days on end, woken to be poked and prodded with different needles and strapped down to a manky hospital bed. I felt like that was where I was going to die, in that manky hospital bed, just like the poor girl who was brought into us over the weekend.

The crazy Doctor clearly didn't know the girl had health problems and without medication, she was left to have seizure after seizure until the last one finished her off. I watched on as the girl thrashed around the bed for ages, then suddenly she just stopped. No movement at all, and it was obvious she had just passed away. The worst part of it all was, no one seemed to bat an eyelid. Leanne and I watched on with horror, knowing that could have been our own fates. The other girls were able to sleep through the ordeal, luckily for them. I had a feeling that moment was going to haunt me for the rest of my life.

***

    I panicked when I woke only to find that my eyes had been covered up again. I was no longer in the hospital bed, and it felt like I was on a boat in choppy waters, then I heard the sound of rubber wheels rubbing and squeaking against a tiled floor. The vibration as the two materials clash together had me jolt upright, only to realise, I was the one in the wheelchair and I had no idea where I was being taken, *was I about to be murdered after all?*
    The Scottish guard had told me I was extremely lucky that the Doc hadn't already had me killed off the second she found out I was pregnant, but maybe that was because she already had a buyer in mind for both me and my unborn baby. I tried to not think about that too much, the stress alone was making me feel like I could throw up at any given second. Morning sickness wasn't nice, and no one warns you that you can have the nauseating feeling throughout the entire day. *So why do they call it morning sickness?*
    Whoever was steering the wheelchair needed to redo their driving licence as I was swung from one corridor to another. The air felt sharp against my face,

and I felt like my driver was walking with some haste. I was swung from left and right as the person pushing me started to speed up even more. Then a loose tile or something on the floor had the front wheel buckle under itself and I was almost tipped out onto the floor. Thankfully, I was strapped in, and whoever was controlling the chair, managed to keep me from face planting the floor.

During all the commotion I heard raised voices, like someone was being manhandled and almost falling out of the chair meant my blindfold had slipped down from my eye, not completely but enough to see part of my surroundings. I was shocked to see that we were still in the hospital but the room we'd just passed was a canteen with tables and chairs, then we passed an office and another room filled with empty hospital beds. I kept my head down, so the guard didn't realise I could see, but I was scanning everything in an attempt to catch a glimpse of something that could help me figure out where we were. We passed a second office which was occupied, and I swear I recognised the girl behind the desk.

Was that Jenny? Maybe I was seeing things, but I was almost certain I just caught sight of Jenny or at least her double. Although it couldn't have been Jenny, she didn't look as unkept or neglected as the rest of us, the girl behind the desk looked dressed to the nines. She was dressed to work in an office, with clean styled hair, a far cry from the girl held in the concrete cell with the rest of us. That place was getting stranger by the day.

Seamus cleared his throat; I knew that cough from a mile away. Even though he had told me he would protect me, it was hard to trust him but how could anyone trust in that place. I wanted to look around to confirm what I'd expected but I was scared. If it wasn't the friendly guard, I would've given myself away, and I had the upper hand being able to see out of half an eye.

I had no idea where I was being taken, maybe I was about to be killed off just like he'd warned me. Either way I was about to find out my fate. We were walking down a long poorly lit corridor when Seamus stopped and removed a pair of keys from his trouser pocket, the sound of him opening a door, echoed in the hallway and moments later I was wheeled into a small room. The room didn't have much lighting in it so I couldn't see very well but it looked like I was wheeled into a storeroom. I heard the door shut behind us and felt the weight lift from the push bars at the back of wheelchair. Then he lowered himself to my, half an eye, level.

There was no hiding the fact that I could see him. My heartrate increased as I had no way of recovering my eyes and the last time I was caught peaking, I was starved for a whole week and put on an intervenes drip to keep me alive and that was the last thing I needed being pregnant. It wasn't only my own life in danger, but my unborn child's too and up until that point, I was ready to give up, but something was giving me a glimmer of hope, and I guessed it was the baby.

The guard noticed my blindfold had slipped, but instead of covering my face up again, he removed it completely. *Maybe he was trying to help me.*

"Where am I?" I asked.

"In the old storeroom. You'll be safe here, but you need to stay hidden little one, Crazy Doc is on one today and the shit is really hitting the fan." Seamus whispered. "Promise me you'll stay here!"

"It's not as if I have much choice." I muttered. "How long are you keeping me in this cupboard?" I asked but he just told me I needed to keep quiet.

"If she hears you, she will have you killed this time!" He warned.

"Have me killed? I thought you talked her around?"

"Little one, you know I tried, she almost had away with me for even mentioning it. She can't sell a pregnant lass."

"So that is why we've been taken, to be sold?"
"I shouldn't have said anything." He sounded worried. "I need to get you away from here, before she finds you."

"And how to you expect to do that?" I asked sarcastically.

"I am working on it, please just stay here, I will be back in a minute."

Was he trying to rescue me?

I wanted to believe him, I wanted to trust him. I was a prisoner and needed his help, after all he had his own lanyard and set of keys. Maybe I could have stolen his set of keys and made a run for it myself, although that was very doubtful. I was tied to the wheelchair so it wasn't as if I could have just walked out of the place, and I felt weak, very weak.

I tried to wiggle my wrist free, but was no use, the cable ties just rubbed against my skin, making my wrists sore to the point they were starting to bleed. My legs were tied just as tight, so I was still as trapped as ever.

Ten minutes or so passed when I heard raised voices in the corridor, as if an argument was taking place, it was hard to hear properly but I could tell it was the Scottish guard arguing with someone. I couldn't hear the other person, but it sounded like he was being reprimanded again because I heard him apologise a few times before saying he'll be right on it. I was scared that whoever was taking to Seamus was about to enter the storeroom and catch me, so I stayed as quiet as possible.

I listened in as the corridor fell silent once again. I was terrified and just wanted it all to end. Not as in end my life, knowing I was pregnant had taken away any of those suicidal thoughts because my baby was going to need a mother.

All of a sudden, I felt a twinge in my lower stomach which had me pulling on my wrists again. I'd had a few little aches and pains here and there, but nothing that I believed was anything serious. If anything, they'd been less painful than my normal monthly cramps, so I was confident my baby was a little fighter, just like their mummy. Although that didn't stop me worrying that all the stress would somehow be harmful for my baby. It couldn't continue. I knew that I needed to escape, and I knew my best option was to put some of my trust into Seamus, but it seemed hopeless, I was bound to a wheelchair and locked in a small room. *Even if I'd escaped the chair, how on earth was I going to get out of the prison?* Whether I liked it or not, I needed his help, but did that mean that I had to trust him too?

A few moments passed; I was in deep thought when I heard the unmistakeable sound of the psycho doctors heels against the tiled floor just outside the door. Seamus had told me the storeroom was quiet and there was no way I would be found because the room was very rarely used. He didn't tell me that the corridor outside was going to be a meeting point for everyone. The doctor's footsteps were becoming clearer, and indication she was walking towards the storeroom. Next I heard the door handle shake, but thankfully it was locked, and she didn't sound like she was reaching for a set of keys either. If she'd have found me in there, she would have gone ape shit and no doubt, she'd have killed me off, once and for all.

Voices were muffled on the other side of the door, as the doctor stopped to talk to someone.

"Jennifer did you sort out the ward for the new girls?" The doctor asked.

"Yes, it is all ready for the new batch." The person responded.

I recognise that voice.

I knew deep down that there was something off with Jenny, and that moment said it all to me. She was a double-crossing cow who was working with the crazy doctor the whole time; I wouldn't have been surprised if Jenny was the one tricking the young girls and trying to make them trust her, making it easier for the guards to abduct them. I wouldn't put anything past anyone in that place.

"Yes mother." Her voice was unmistakeable, that moany teenage response was definitely Jenny's.

What didn't make sense, was Jenny being the crazy doctor's daughter. Why was she held in a cell with the rest of us girls? Like what mother would do that to their own child?

I heard Jenny sigh again before questioning the doctor. "Are you sure this is the right thing to do mum? I am worried because Andrew has been threatening to go to the police?"

"Andrew will not be saying a word. I have sorted it." The doctor replied.

"I just thought…" Jenny was about to say.

The doctor was clearly annoyed with her daughter and stopped her in mid-sentence. "That is your first problem, I didn't ask you to think, did I?"

"Sorry mother."

My mind was in a spin. I couldn't get over the fact that Jenny was the crazy doctors daughter. But why would she have agreed to be chained up in that concreate box with us for weeks on end? I just couldn't wrap m head around it all, and I was seriously pissed off with Jennifer.

Granted the doctor didn't get her nickname for being a nice and friendly doctor but to treat your own flesh and blood in that way, made me wonder just how fucked up the doctor really was. Unless Jenny being in the box was a setup, a way to make Leanne and myself trust that she was on our side to try and gain information from us. If that was the case it didn't work because I didn't like Jenny and I never gave her any information because I didn't trust her. I would open up to Leanne at times, when Jenny wasn't in the cell with us, but that was about it.

Was Leanne part of the plan too? Was I about to find out that they were all in on it together? As you can imagine my mind was on overdrive.

CHAPTER SIX – The escape artist

Seamus returned about an hour later but I still had no idea what was going on in the man's head. He seemed erratic and scared stiff of us being caught. I just wanted to leave, but Seamus hadn't come to rescue me, if anything I believed he was regretting taking me from my hospital bed, the bed was a lot more comfortable than the wheelchair. I was starting to worry about Seamus, and found it hard to trust he'd help me escape when he was panicking so much. Then he told me I had to stay where I was for another hour at least. I looked at him in shock, another hour may not have been much time at all, but being cold, tried and uncomfortable meant an hour could feel like an entire day. Seamus told me I had no other choice but to stay put, I thought he was saying it to be an arsehole, but informed me he was waiting on the doctor to head home for the night so we could finally make our escape.

Seamus at least removed my restraints, before leaving me alone with nothing but my thoughts. Before closing the door, he told me to wait for him. It wasn't as if I could go anywhere, the door was locked as soon as he left, and it was a solid wooden door with a hefty looking lock that no one was opening without the right key.

I knew needing to pee should have been the last thing on my mind, but I'd been holding it in for over an hour. There was nothing in the room I could have used as a bucket either, apart from the wheelchair and some boxes of office and cleaning supplies, the room was empty. Reluctantly I knew I had no choice but to relieve myself. I lifted myself to my feet, but I was unsteady. I'd been strapped down in a hospital bed for over a week and it took me a few minutes to find the strength to stand. My ankle hurt as I placed the pressure on it, and I almost came crashing down to the floor, but I managed to keep myself upright. It took me a few minutes, but I eventually made my way over to the shelving unit on the back wall. I was desperate to pee, that I felt a dribble trickle down my legs so, I pulled up my nightdress and quickly as I could and crouched down so I could pee in the corner of the room. Having a wee, stung and I wondered if something to do with the baby, or maybe it was all the drugs they had been pumping into me.

  I felt a small sense of achievement, peeing in that corner, it was like I was imagining how pissed off the doctor would have been if she'd known. Heaven forbid any of us girls made a mess in our cell, so she'd have gone nuts at me. That thought alone had me smiling from ear to ear. Pity it wasn't her face I was urinating all over.

  A few hours passed and there was still no sign of the guard, I was left wondering if he'd forgotten about me. I was also frustrated with him because I hadn't managed to get much information out of him and I would've preferred to know what his plan was, instead of being kept in the dark, literally.

  He'd mentioned the doctor thinking I was already dead, so I wouldn't be looked for. The thought of being free from that place had me breaking down in tears, a sign of relief. Another few hours was worth the wait, if I was going to never have to see that place again, pity the same couldn't be said for Seamus, as he was planning to return to work the very next day. As it turned out, I became worthless to the doctor pregnant. Which I would have thought she'd make even more on a newborn baby, she could have had two of us for the price of one, but Seamus told me it was because I was only thirteen years old and the doctor wouldn't allow me to be sold, as it didn't sit right with her. It seemed our psychotic doctor had some misplaced morals.

My stomach was aching for food because I hadn't eaten in almost twenty-four hours, which would have been fine, if I didn't have a baby sucking all the life out of me. I had become accustomed to the regular mealtimes and as much as I was sick to the back teeth of sandwiches, I would have eaten a thousand of them at that point.

***

I was woken to the sound of the lock mechanism opening, and went to bolt upright but with truly little energy and feeling sick to my stomach, I couldn't move. I was annoyed with myself for drifting off and I was in a bit of a daze. I might have only dozed off for a few minutes, but that was a few minutes too long. The door opened and the small storeroom was engulfed in bright sunlight. It was night-time when Seamus left me in the room, so I must've slept through the entire night.

I tried to remain quiet in the corner of the tiny room. My heart started racing and fear took over me as I prayed that I wouldn't be noticed by the young woman in a nurses outfit who'd just appeared in the doorway. My prayers weren't answered as the nurse looked directly in my direction. A worried expression took over what I could see of her face, she shushed at me to keep quiet and closed the door behind her.

The room was in darkness again, but I could see the nurse as sheepishly approached me. I wasn't sure what to expect and I braced myself, I was in the corner of the tiny storeroom with back was against the wall, it was cold, and the fear of the unknown made me shudder.

"You shouldn't be in here." She whispered.

No shit sherlock. I thought, I had tried to speak but no words left my lips, my throat was dry and scratchy.

"Oh, poor you, do you need some water?" She asked.

I nodded in response and then I was passed a bottle of unopened water, that she'd just removed from her overall pocket. She said she'd just purchased it from the drinks machine in the canteen and that I was welcome to it. I thanked her and reached for the bottle, but I had no strength to open it. I didn't need to say anything because it was as if she could read my mind. She removed the bottle from my hands and opened it for me. Instead of passing it back, she moved closer so she could place the water bottle against my lips. I was more that grateful and never realised just how refreshing water could be, it was like I had never tasted water so good in my life and I couldn't get enough of it. I felt my nightdress getting drenched with the water missing my lips, but I didn't care, it was worth it.

I thanked the nurse, before she screwed the lid back on the bottle and placed it on the floor next to my feet.

"What time is it?" I asked.

"Just gone nine in the morning. Have you been locked in here all night?" she asked.

I had no idea what to say to her in response, I didn't trust anyone, and I was scared stiff of saying the wrong thing to the wrong person. I wanted to trust her, and spent a few seconds looking deeply into her eyes and hoping that would tell me if her intentions were pure or not. It didn't but I tried to convince myself otherwise.

What was the worst that could happen? She could have ran straight to the doctor. Worst case scenario. the doctor found out about me and ordered my killing. That was a bounty I already had over my head, so what did I have to lose?

"I am getting out of here with any luck," I said but the nurse smirked at me, "you don't understand, I'm pregnant so no longer of any use to the doctor. She wants me dead, so someone is helping me escape." I explained.

"Escape? But you can't." The nurse looked at me in horror and I instantly regretted being so honest with her.

"Did you not hear the part when I mentioned I am pregnant?"

She remained silent for a few minutes, I saw the cogs going around in her mind and then she informed me that one of the guards were caught the night before, and the rumour was the Doctor had him taken care of. Taken care of, usually meant one thing in that prison – Death.

"I can't see you escaping love, and you can't keep hiding in here, this room is used far too much. You need to go back to your bed."

"I don't have a bed." I explained, "She thinks I am dead already." I reminded her.

"I don't know what you expect, but no one is helping you escape, it wouldn't be worth their while. I could be reprimanded for just for talking to you!"
She spent the next few minutes panicking; and eventually she advised me to stay put and remain as quiet as possible. *What other choice did I have?*

"I really should mention this to my supervisor, but I worry what that would mean for the both of us." She warned. "You need to leave here; you can't stay in this room."

The last thing I wanted was for anyone else to get into any trouble because of me and I told her to just forget she had ever seen me,

"I am going to be either dead or gone from this place soon enough." I reminded her.

She then had the cheek to tell me it was her job to protect us girls above anything else.

"Protect us?" I laughed in her face. "Not one person in this messed up place has protected us. We have been abducted to be sold off, they are trafficking us, so please tell me how the hell you can call that protection?"

I was angry at her remark and my voice was slightly raised which had her stressing even more.

"Please, keep it down, you are going to get us both in hot water." She warned. "You don't understand, we do what we have to do, in order to survive. Half of us, are just as trapped as you girls."

"Clearly." I muttered.

How the hell was she in the same position as me? She was delusional to even compare our situations and the more she tried to reason with me, the angrier I became. Seamus had the cheek to tell me the same thing, but like I'd said to him, I didn't see them all being chained up, or strapped to a bed. The staff at that place may have had some form of hold over them to make them do the horrific things they were doing, but they were anything but in the same boat as me.

"Just leave me alone, please."

Thankfully, she listened to me and got back up to her feet, she was about to walk towards the storeroom door when she turned around to ask if I had eaten.
I hadn't eaten any food for over twenty-four hours, and I was starving. She told me she'd return with some breakfast for me, but warned me to hide in the corner as the cleaner was due to restock the storeroom around midday.

"I will be back before then with your food. Don't go anywhere." She whispered.

Like why did everyone keep saying that to me? I wasn't going anywhere.
The nurse opened the door and peeked her head around the corner to make sure the coast was clear before leaving. I noticed she didn't lock the door and I was left wondering if she'd done it with the intention of giving me a chance to escape myself. From the information I received from the nurse, it sounded like my saviour couldn't even save himself from the doctor wrath, never mind save me. *Did she have Seamus killed off?*

I pulled myself up to my feet, but my legs didn't feel like they were attached to me anymore. Not like pins and needles, but almost as if my brain had forgotten to send the signal down to my legs, like they were missing a connection. I used every ounce of upper body strength and eventually I was stood upright, leaning my fragile body up against the wall for stability. A few seconds passed before I started to gain any feeling in my toes again, a little while longer before the feelings returned to my feet.

Slowly I attempted to take a step forward, still using the wall to support my upper body, but it was a struggle, and I almost lost my footing. I leant forward holding onto to metal shelving unit which covered the majority of the back wall. It was dark in the room, but my eyes had adjusted to the lack of light enough to see my surroundings, but not well enough as I lost my footing for the second time and found myself stumbling backwards and landing on my butt. My body went crashing towards to the ground causing me to knock over one of the boxes filled with biro pens. A bunch of plastic pens falling from shoulder height in a small, compact room make an almighty racket.

"Shit!"

I was sure someone would have heard me, *Why is that always the way? When you try and be quiet, you make even more noise.* That was definitely one of those occasions.

It took me a few minutes but once I'd calmed myself down, I found myself stood opposite the storeroom door. *This was it, my way out,* I thought but my stupid body had other ideas, instead of walking towards the door, my knees buckled beneath me again. I didn't know what was wrong with me and feared I was dying or something, it felt like my body was shutting down on me. Had I been in the right frame of mind, it would've been obvious that I was weak because my legs hadn't been used in weeks and nothing more, but I wasn't thinking straight and fear had my body reaching a state of panic, my breathing became a struggle, and I knew what was happening. I was having a panic attack.

I'd had panic attacks in primary school, and the tightness in my chest, felt terribly similar. Ideally I needed a paper bag to help get my breathing back on an even keel, but there was nothing in the room that resembled a bag.

"I can't do this." I muttered to myself helplessly. Tears flowing down my cheeks. Silent tears because I didn't want to be heard.

I was sure I was going to die in that room, but I wasn't quite ready to give up the fight. Then I remembered the water bottle and realised I may have been able to use that instead of a bag. I emptied the water onto the floor, not caring where it spilt and placed the empty bottle to my lips, using it as a breathing aid. Someone up in heaven was answering my prayer because it worked and within minutes my breathing was normalised and the pain in my chest had eased.

I realised in that moment, just how foolish I was to even think I could escape on my own, I could just about walk, never mind bolt it if I needed to. I was feeling weak and defeated, completely defeated and I'd started to believe my only option was to hand myself in, maybe the doctor would have felt sorry for me and let me live. It was doubtful but I had hoped by explaining a guard took me against my will, she'd be softer on me. It seemed like it was my only way out.

Just as I was about to give up and hand myself over to the crazy doctor, the door handle moved. I was sure I was about to be caught and I resigned myself to the fact that I had lost and being dead meant it would at least all be over. The door opened and I was relieved and surprised to see Seamus. He looked at me and I sighed in relief. I was a little shocked to see him, considering I was under the impression he was caught, and dealt with and I was glad to see him standing in front of me, but I was seriously annoyed at him for leaving me in the storeroom overnight with no explanation

"You are still here." He said as he closed the door and locked it behind him.
At least he was observant.

I noticed his voice had an air of panic to it, maybe he'd hoped I had already been caught, that way I wouldn't be his problem anymore and he could just get on with his merry little life. I wouldn't be anyone's problem ever again.

"Well, where else did you expect me to be?" I replied sarcastically, miffed that he was hoping otherwise. "Disappointed?" I asked.

"No, it's just, the door was unlocked; I didn't think you'd still be in here given half a chance, I thought you'd have been away a long time ago."

I didn't want to tell him, I couldn't physically move, and that I had tried to escape. Whether I liked it or not, I needed him.

"What took you so long?" I asked. "You were meant to come back for me last night. I had to piss in the corner of the room, and I've had no food for an entire day. I'm starving and pissed off with you."

He went on to tell me that he was sent on an errand for the crazy doctor, so he wasn't able to return like he'd agreed but told me, he'd made arrangements for us to leave, but we would have to go soon.

"Arrangements?" I asked.

Seamus just looked at me and winked, it frustrated me because he refused to go into details and told me I didn't need to worry about anything, as he had everything under control. He made a comment about the less I knew, the safer I would be. Then he told me he needed to make a phone call first and assured me that we would both be away from that hellhole in no time. I wanted to trust him, but my mind was all over the place and I didn't find it in me to trust anyone, and who could have blamed me. I felt sick to my stomach and had zero energy to argue, let alone fight anyone so, I was willing to do whatever than man had said, just for it all to be over and done with.

"I need food." I said, pretty abruptly but I didn't care how I came across to him, I was hangry, and it was Seamus's fault, if he hadn't locked me in a storeroom for twenty-four hours, then I wouldn't be feeling so ill. Although if Seamus had left me in that hospital bed, I doubt I wouldn't have still been alive.

"The nurse said she'd bring me some breakfast, but she was just as bad as you. She abandoned me too, said she'd…"

I was interrupted mid-sentence as Seamus grabbed hold of the top of my arms and shook me. "Who?" He looked at me in horror. "No one can know you are here, otherwise my whole plan is ruined. Who was she, what nurse?" He spat his words at me, it was clear I'd angered him.

I spent the next five minutes trying to calm the man down. I went on to explain what had happened that morning, but he was just telling me off.

"I thought you weren't coming back." I stated.

I was under the impression he'd gone AWOL, but Seamus didn't want to listen to me, no matter how much I tried to calm him down, he was clearly worried and shitting himself. He started asking me question after question, trying to determine which nurse had caught me.

He reckoned he needed to intervene before we were both in serious trouble. My answers gave him no clarity and considering there were a fair few nurses helping to run the place, I wasn't surprised. She could have been anyone, plus they all looked exactly the same in their uniforms and surgical white masks. He didn't like that response, but I defended myself, explaining that I believed she was my only option to escape, what with him apparently being dead and all that.

"Anyway, I was told you were dead." I snapped.

He looked at me bewildered; a small crackle leaving his lips. "You are on about Jonny." He paused, "The bloke shouldn't have been caught sleeping with the girls then. If he kept it in his pants, he would still have his manhood. Serves him right."

A little hypercritical if you'd asked me, although I was in no position to argue with him. He was trying to help me escape and I was being a complete and utter cow to him.

"I still need to find out who else knows about you, I will be back as soon as I can."

"But my food..."

Seamus looked back at me, pulling his finger up to his lips, to signal that I needed to keep quiet and then he left the storeroom and me, yet again. With no way out because he's locked to door behind him.

"Great, this is all I need!" defeated again, I sat down in the wheelchair, it was warmer than the tiled floor.

CHAPTER SEVEN – My getaway

It felt like another day had passed as I was dipping in and out of sleep, too weak to stay alert. It hadn't but I was becoming increasingly impatient. I felt a tiredness I had never experienced in the past, I was sure that the baby growing inside me had me feeling weaker than normal, the poor little thing was no doubt screaming out for some subsidence just as much as I was. I was just so tired, physically, and emotionally and I was starting to lose every ounce of hope, waiting on a man returning to rescue me. I honestly believed I was going to die in that room and so much for the storeroom being in constant use, since Seamus went off trying to find out who saw me, not one person had tried to enter. I guessed the nurse only told me that to scare me into leaving the storeroom, I suppose it was easier for everyone if I was gone.

When Seamus returned, he was being very bossy with me, he refused to answer any of my questions and snapped at me.

"I am trying to help you; you could sound a little bit more grateful." He said, "I could have just left you to die. Now do ask you are told, before a change my mind!"

I was told to cover my face and to get back into the wheelchair. At first I wanted to argue with him, but I needed his help. Once I was sat down and in the chair, he informed me that he had food waiting for us both in his van, I just needed to trust him and do exactly as he said. I wave of relief washed over me at the thought of freedom again and I obviously done as I was asked.

"I won't strap you in, but you need to not move a muscle. Do you hear me little one?"

I nodded my head in agreement as he covered up my face with one of those dreaded pillowcases. At least it was a clean one, I could smell the washing powder again, which reminded me of my grandmother, and it gave me a small sense of comfort, just like it had done, months before. Knowing I was soon going to be away from that place had me excitedly moving about in the chair and I was rewarded with a clip around the back of the head and told to keep still.

"Any stupid moves like that, and I won't be taking you anywhere." He warned.

The feeling of cold metal on my legs had them jolting out in front of me, but I was warned again to keep as still as possible.

"It wasn't my fault," I stated.

"Silence now, or we will both be in big trouble. Normally when moving you girls, you'd be drugged up, so don't make me regret not drugging you."

The way he spoke about it baffled me; it was like drugging up little girls was a normal daily occurrence to him. *How many girls did he have the pleasure of moving?* As much as I wanted to trust Seamus, it didn't make any sense him helping me, unless he had feelings for me. I really hoped that wasn't the case because I didn't like him in that way. He was the only half decent person in that place, hence why I spoke with him. The rest of the guards were scary, so it wasn't as if I'd had much choice.

The light penetrated the fabric as the storeroom was door opened fully and Seamus started wheeling me out, into the corridor. I had a hundred different questions running through my mind, wondering if he'd caught up with the nurse and if so what was said, wondering how he could just wheel me out of that hellhole without looking suspicious, *what was the catch?* As Seamus wheeled me down what I presumed was an awfully long corridor, a few members of staff greeted him. I couldn't understand how so many people could act so normal in that situation. I was apparently an unconscious girl, being held captive like many others but not one person batted an eyelid. It was messed up.

I started wondering what was going to happen to me when we did escape. How did Seamus know where to drop me off? Maybe he was going to take me to the at the same place I was abducted from, but the school was usually busy and far too public to release me, without being spotted. Surly.

I wanted to know what the plan was, but I was kept in the dark and hated that I didn't have all of the answers.

I wasn't sure where I would go once Seamus released me, because I couldn't got home to my parents, my father was going to go ballistic when he caught hold of me, regardless of my reasons, I had been missing for over seven weeks and he was sure to make me pay for my actions. That's before he finds out his thirteen-year-old daughter is pregnant, I doubt I would be pregnant for long, not if he got his hands on me.

Maybe I would be better off on my own anyway and I was never going to be on my own, I would be with my baby. I wasn't scared of being a mum, and told myself, that if could handle the last two months, I was going to handle anything motherhood threw at me.

Time slowed down dramatically as I was being wheeled down what seemed like a never-ending corridor, turning from left to right. I was sure we were travelling in a circle at one point. The place I called my prison must've been a massive building. A private hospital maybe? *How could the place be that big in size, yet stay hidden from the authorities, it didn't make any sense.*

I was dragged out of my own thoughts when all of a sudden we stopped dead in our tracks, my instincts were to ask why we'd stopped, but I kept my mouth shut and my body as still as possible, after all I was meant to be unconscious.

I heard a door being opened in front of us and my heart started beating even faster, *was I nearly free?* I finally understood the saying "smelling your freedom," as the fresh, clean air touched my fore arms and legs for the first time in weeks.

I held onto my breath as I felt Seamus lean down towards me, he whispered to me to tell me that we were almost at his van. I smiled to myself and started to wonder what freedom was going to look like, I was nervous but also excited. The air was cold, and with the lack of food my body, I started to tremble. Seamus hissed at me, but there wasn't much I could do about it, it wasn't as if I was doing it on propose. I was finding it extremely hard to sit still and act lifeless.

"We are almost at the van, just stay still." He whispered. "You need to act dead."

My head was already slumped to one side, I just needed to keep still, just then I heard voices approaching us.

"Is this the girl going to the Davis's?" A man shouted over towards our direction.

"Yes Sir. Delivery for 5pm." Seamus replied.

"Perfect, you best get going, traffic is a nightmare today."

I understood Seamus's escape plan finally, he was pretending I was one of his deliveries. It looked like the Davis family were going to be disappointed when their delivery didn't materialise but that wasn't my responsibility. We slopped down and then came to a stop. I assumed we were at the back of the van as I heard the doors opening, followed by a big clonk as the ramp was being lowered. A gust of wind from the ramp hitting the floor lifted the front of my stupid frilly nightgown and my knees knocked against each other involuntary. I was grateful when I felt myself being wheeled into the back of the van, a wave of pure relief washed over me, but it was short lived.

"She just moved." The male voice shouted.

"Are you sure that wasn't just the way you are getting her in?" Seamus asked trying to cover his tracks.

"No, I am sure. She moved."

I thought Seamus had wheeled me into the van and worried that the new bloke was about to mess up the whole escape plan. My wheelchair was stationed, and the brakes applied. Then I felt a hand near my shoulder as the pillowcase was lifted. I stayed as still as possible and thankfully my eyes were closed. Maybe he was checking to see if I was awake, but I'd believed I had convinced him enough when I felt him move away from me. He muttered something in a foreign language as his voice travelled further away. Then I heard his footsteps approaching me again and by that point, I could feel my heart beating hard in my chest, I was sure we were about to be caught.

"Jason, you are useless, the girl isn't even strapped in." The man scolded Seamus, telling him how useless he was, which you could tell was getting my rescuers back up.

"I am sure she's fine; she is knocked out." Seamus said trying to defuse the situation. "Just leave it, she's my responsibility."

That wasn't the first time I'd heard those words leave his lips.

It took all my inner strength not to move as I felt hands on me. Regardless of Seamus's attempts to stop it happening, my arms and legs were strapped to the wheelchair. I then felt what seems to be a seatbelt placed around my stomach. For the first time in my life, I worried that the seatbelt was too tight for my baby bump. I was surprised my little Jellybean was still alive in there, but with no signs of anything, I only had my gut instincts to go on, and the child belonged to me, so they were sure to be a little fighter.

"You really need to check they are strapped in next time, what happens if the wee bitch woke and done a runner?" Seamus was asked.

"They are drugged up, and I haven't known a girl run yet." Seamus replied sarcastically.

I was all too aware that I wasn't to move a muscle, but the unknown man was rough with me and pitched the skin on my wrist, I couldn't help but hiss, but thankfully he didn't hear me because he was too busy arguing with Seamus. The man was clearly taking his frustrations with my rescuer out on me instead.

"Right, she is secured now. Don't be sloppy next time."

"Sorry Boss, I won't." Seamus replied and both men started laughing between themselves.

"Are you watching the big game this week?" Seamus was asked and him and the other bloke starting talking about football.

The van doors were slammed shut and I was in complete darkness yet again. I could still hear the two of them talking but I was thankful that I was on my own and couldn't be seen. I wasn't impressed with being strapped into place though. Another ten minutes passed before the van started up and I was able to finally let out a sigh of relief, but I was annoyed with Seamus, and I felt sick as the vehicle rumbled beneath me. Seamus hadn't given me the food he'd promised either. It was an extremely uncomfortable van journey as the whole time I had to stop was about myself from throwing up in the pillowcase, and my bladder was full again. Every bump in the road had me squeezing my thighs together.

"Hey Jason." I shouted but he couldn't hear me over the sound of the engine. So, I shouted again, even louder.

"Oi, Jason."

He replied to me by hitting the metal barrier between us and telling me to keep quiet. Although he wasn't as polite with his words.

"You promised me food!"

"Shut it little one." He shouted again. "Or I will be forced to shut you up myself."

Instantly I heard the tone of his voice change, and I could tell the man was derailing, and friendship I believed we had. He was pissed off with me for using his name and shouted just as much. I'm sure he didn't want his name to get out, but I couldn't unhear it and so I repeatedly called his name. Nevertheless, I was ignored.

I shook my head from side to side, until the pillowcase finally fell from my face. I was in pure darkness, but I knew that if I could've just loosen the straps holding me in place then I could untie myself and give myself more of a fighting chance of getting out of the van. The tone of my drivers voice had me realising I couldn't trust him, something was going on and I didn't know what, but I knew being strapped to that wheelchair wasn't going to help. I wriggled with what little energy I had but it was no use. The man who'd strapped me to the wheelchair done a great job in doing so, I was not getting out of that chair without help. So yet again, my fate was in Jason's hands. I still preferred the nickname I'd given him but knowing his name was really pissing him off and the man lied to me time and time again, so I wanted to annoy him.

"Jason, I need the toilet." I shouted but instead of responding to me, he turned the radio up full blast in an attempt to drown me out. I was so disappointed in the man and myself for trusting him. I was under the impression he was helping me but soon realised, I had been played, he made sure I trusted him so I would leave the hospital with him. *But why? What did he have planned for me?* Whatever it was, I wasn't convinced it was going to be much fun.

I zoned out to the music although it wasn't my cup of tea. Any music was welcoming after listening to girls screaming and the rattling of chains for two months. It was as if the odd heavy metal tracks held resemblance to the house of horrors I'd just escaped from, very haunting. How heavy metal became so popular, I will never understand but it was no surprise Jason was into that type of music, he looked like he'd appreciate a good mosh pit.

Spice girls came on the radio just as he van came to a stop, typical that the only song I recognised from his playlist would come on just as we reached our destination. Suddenly I felt overly nervous and scared. Not knowing what was going to happen next had me struggling to keep what little contents of my stomach left inside me. Pity I hadn't managed to have the same control over my bladder, I was sat drenched in my own urine, I did try and warn him that I needed a pee, but I was ignored.

The radio was still blasting Piccadilly Key 103 so I knew we were still in the city of Manchester but where abouts, I couldn't have told you. Not that it was going to matter if I was about to be killed off, that was my biggest worry, that Jason was taking me away from the compound to murder me. The engine stopped, turning off the music with it and then I heard him getting out of the driver's side of the vehicle and I automatically started panicking. Knowing my fate was in his hands, scared me a little more than the being with the crazy doctor, at least I knew what to expect with her, Jason on the other hand, fooled me into thinking he was on my side.

I knew that if I wasn't strapped into the damn wheelchair, I might have had a fighting chance, but I was just as trapped as ever, and I could hear Jason approaching the back of the van. I held onto my breath.

The van doors opened, and Jason was stood there, he made the mistake of not putting his ski mask back on, he would have assumed my head was still covered with the pillowcase. He looked different without the mask on, scary almost with a menacing look on his face. It was a look I had seen on others faces, but not a look I would have placed on his and I was fearful of him.

"You said you would let me go. You are meant to be helping me escape, please Jason, please." I pleaded with him as he made his way towards me.

"I cannot do that little one, but I've made another arrangement for you, and you'll be a lot safer where you're going."

"Please Jason, please let just me go."

He looked me dead in the eyes, "You know too much, and you'll run straight to the police, I am not going to jail for this shit Princess."

"I won't tell a soul, I promise, I won't." I begged but to no avail.

Just then I notice he had a needle in his hands, and I begged him to leave me alone.

"I promise you, one hundred percent, I won't tell anyone what happened. Please just let me go." I screamed out as Jason took hold of my forearm.

"No can do little one, I am sorry." I swear he smiled at me, and I felt my blood start to boil.

"You ain't sorry in the slightest, you are just as messed up as that psycho doctor. You are all sick and twisted bastards."

The needle penetrated my skin regardless of how much I had tried to wiggle free. Jason had told me he didn't want to harm me, but that was exactly what he'd done, he'd betrayed me and that is what hurt me the most.
Within seconds my eyes felt heavy, and I was gone.

CHAPTER EIGHT – My new home

I Felt groggy as hell and sick to my stomach as I opened my eyes reluctantly, I was scared of seeing my new surroundings, but I could tell I was laid down on an old springy mattress, the springs digging into my side, were the giveaway. The air smelt musky and the blanket by my feet was that scratchy type of material your grandmother probably owned during the war. It was going to irritate my skin, but at least I wasn't dead. Silver linings and all that.

"Goody, you are awake."

A male voice spoke, which had me jumping out of my skin. I attempted to move my head, but I struggled, my body felt heavy and limp. The male voice told me not to move and assured me I was safe with him. I wanted to see who was talking to me, but he was stood too far away for me to catch a glimpse.

"I am here to look after you." He said, sounding pretty cheery.

Moments passed as I dipped in and out of consciousness, but I could hear the man walking around me. Just then I caught a glimpse of his worn-out jeans and an overused brown, leather belt. Extra holes were made in the leather which told me the man had been putting on the pounds since buying the belt.

It's stupid the unimportant things our minds capture.

"You need some food, you look starving." He said and then persisted to ask me what foods I liked, but rather than waiting for me to answer him, he was guessing my answers himself.

It was beyond frustrating. I was asked if I liked pasta, and before I had chance to answer, I was told I had to like pasta, because every young woman liked the stuff, then he started telling me meaningless statistics about the average person's favourite foods, like I cared what other people liked. I was trying to figure out where Jason had dumped me, why would I have cared about how many people in the UK liked a Korma curry, I really didn't. He carried on talking regardless. I had a feeling the man liked to talk.

He walked closer to me, and I found the strength to sit upright to create some distance between us, but he assured me he wasn't going to harm me. I was then helped to my feet, but I was unsteady and needed to rest my weight on the strange man's shoulders. I wondered where he was taking me, and what he wanted from me, but I didn't fight him off, I didn't have an ounce of energy left to fight and resigned myself to whatever was about to happen.

I was surprised as he helped me over to the small wooden table on the far end of the room, it looked like an old table with two wooden framed, matching chairs. They looked worn-out with an old-fashioned print on the cushioned chairs, they were well used and even had bum grooves from whoever used them before me. I called the place old-fashioned because the furniture was remarkably similar to my grandmothers furniture back in the 80s, old and dated and the room smelt old too, damp, and musty. Either that or my nose was super sensitive since finding out I was pregnant.

    I wondered if the man helping to the table, knew I was pregnant, I was sure Jason would have mentioned it when selling me on.

    The table was set out of two, so he was clearly expecting me, and I wondered how long Jason had known he was going to sell me. Once seated I looked up at the balding, middle-aged man and asked him what he expected of me. He just looked at me blackly, his pale blue eyes burrowed into my soul and sent a cold shiver down my spine. Something about him creeped me out, but I couldn't put my finger on it.

    "Where am I?" I asked but the fear of the unknown meant the words struggled to leave my lips. He understood me fine.

    "Home, you are finally home." He said joyfully before placing a napkin on my knees.

    It was at that point I realised I had been dressed up in a pink frilly dress. *What was it with these people and playing dress-up?* Dresses were never my thing, and I wouldn't have been seen dead in one usually. To make matter worse, the dress I'd been paced in was something right out of a fifties movie and as old=fashioned as everything else I was seeing around me. I reached my hand up because I felt something around my neck to find out that I was wearing a beaded necklace, a bit like fake pearls but pink in colour. My hair was placed in a bun on top of my head, and I had a pair of clip-on earrings dangling from each earlobe, which I assumed matched the awful necklace around my neck. I didn't see a mirror, but I could tell I had been dressed up like a bloody doll, which I thought was pretty weird in itself.

As long as he didn't expect me to be his sex doll, it had to be better than being held prisoner in that concreate cell.

"What do you want with me?" I asked, scared of what I was about to hear. *Had he paid for me?*

The man just smiled at me, and told me to sit tight and keep quiet. He told me that if I behaved like a good girl he'd return with our dinner. The thought of food had my mouth watering, and I decided the multitude of questions running around my mind could wait, until my belly was full at least.

The man walked just out of sight before I heard the instinctive sound of a lock being opened, seconds later, I heard the door creak open.

"Back in a mo." He shouted back to me; he sounded a little too chirpy for my liking and then I heard a door slamming shut behind him, and the door being relocked.

As soon as the door closed, I was on my feet. Admittedly a little unsteady but that was to be expected when I'd been sedated and starved of food for days on end. I used the table to steady my body against and took a small step forwards, making it easier to see the rest of the room. I needed to know where I was being held.

I was in what looked like a rundown bedsit. Almost nineteen eighties vibe with its worn-out patterned wallpaper. It looked like someone had tried to divide the room into sections. A brown patterned rug sat beside the bed and another rug under the table which was just as ghastly. In the one corner of the bedroomed area was the single bed complete with the springy, hard mattress I woke up on. A small chest of drawers sat next to the bed and a wardrobe next to that. The other side of the room had a small kitchenette area, with ripped lino and a burn mark which looked like it had a hot pan melt the floor, *at least I had my own cooker* I thought to myself and an old, rusted fridge. I was locked up in a self-contained bedsit, which was a massive upgrade to the concrete cell I'd just escaped from.

Jason was wrong about one thing; I didn't see how I could feel any safer there, when the middle-aged man creeped me out more than the guards ever did. I could only imagine what was about to happen and what he wanted from me.

The bedroom didn't have any windows, so I assumed I was in a basement, the only natural light source was a small skylight which looked like it was housed in a metal cage. Everything looked old and dated. It was like I was transported back in time, which was creepy.

I steadied myself on the edge of the table, before taking another step forward. I wanted to see the door that was keeping me captive, and I regretted looking straight away when I realised the door was made of metal. If I didn't think I was a prisoner before, that door proved I most definitely was.

If the creepy middle-aged man weren't into stealing girls, why would he have a high security door inside his home. It definitely wasn't the type of door you'd see being used for a bedroom. The place was set up well in advance and I wondered if I was the first girl to be kept in that eerie bedroom. Everything about the place had me feeling on edge, and the not knowing part was screwing with my head.

Noises came from the other side of the metal door as I heard the man arguing with someone, I wondered how many others were in that place and I didn't really want to find out, not before eating something and hopefully finding some strength. With that in mind I stepped back and took my seat at the table. I tried to make it look like I'd been sat there entire time by placing the napkin back on my knee and I waited eagerly for my dinner.

I got a whiff of the food as soon as he opened the door and I had to hand it to him, the food smelt amazing and had my mouth watering. I hadn't smelt a cooked dinner in months, but those months felt like years had passed. The man came into my vision, and he was sporting a massive smile on his face. I didn't know how to take him, so I looked away as he placed my bowl of food on the table in front of me.

"Mind, it's hot." He warned.

"Thank you." I muttered, I was so hungry that I didn't wait to be told, I just started scoffing the stew.

"Are you not eating?" I asked, thinking it was a little weird that he'd only dished up a bowl for me, but he had two places set out at the table.

Were we expecting someone else?

He didn't respond to me, instead he smiled, it was a fake smile which made him look scary. My head was screaming at me to get away from him, something about him was very sinister. I worried that the food was poisoned or something, it seemed like the only explanation. *Is that why he wouldn't eat?*

He must have seen the cogs going around my head at high speed as he assured me his food was safe enough to eat. I'd already eaten three mouthfuls and I was thankful for something other than a cheese sandwich. I hadn't eaten stew in years either and I had forgotten just how tasty it was. My nan cooked stew for us all of the time, when I was a small child, but it wasn't really a dish my father would've allowed in our house, because he couldn't stand his mother-in-law. Why? I couldn't tell you; it was an argument that happened when I was only five years old, but one thing was for sure, knowing my father it would have been over something pretty trivial. That man held onto the stupidest of grudges and enjoyed making a massive point of it. If he felt the need to fall out with someone, everyone knew about it. My nan was no exception.

I was scoffing the stew so fast and hardly chewing it before allowing it to go down my throat, that it was burning my tongue and causing myself indigestion in the process, but my stomach was begging to be fed and I wasn't about to argue with it.

"There is more where that came from, I know it is your favourite dear." He said, looking at me with an intense look on his face, his fake smile turned into a weird, strained look on his face, as if he was holding his breath. He cheeks went red as if he was blushing and then a crackle of a smile left his lips.

Then I realised what he'd said that stew was my favourite meal. The food was nice don't get me wrong, but it was far from my favourite meal. I looked at him confused and then I noticed he had tears in his eyes, like he was about to break down into floods of tears.
Why was he crying? I didn't know how to handle an upset man, so I just looked away and concentrated on my food in front of me. The facial expressions coming from the man were the strangest thing I had ever seen, I didn't know whether the laugh or cry, so staring at my stew was my only option.
"I've waiting so long for you to come home Helen, so, so long. It feels like a lifetime ago since we last ate a meal together."

I didn't want to point out that I was the only person sat at the table eating, he was just staring at me weirdly and crying. *Why was he was calling me Helen?* Maybe Jason gave him a false name when I he sold me to him, it would kind of make sense.

"You were hungry Helen, weren't you?" he asked.

I didn't know why. but being called someone else's name was irritating me.

"My name is Siobhan." I told the man; I was still filling my face with mouthfuls of food, so talking in between spoons. "Siobhan Everdeen Sir, and I need to get back home to my family. My parents will be looking for me, they must be all worried sick."

I knew my parents wouldn't have cared less about me, but I'd hoped in telling my new owner that I had plenty of people out looking for me, he'd have had no option but to let me go.

He didn't even acknowledge that I'd spoken, instead he just carried on staring at me, watching closely as I stuffed my face. There could have been rat poisoning in the gravy for all I knew. That was probably why he had a huge smile plastered over his face again, but it was too late anyway, had that been the case, I'd have already consumed more than enough to of killed me off.

"Can I get you some more?" He asked and I nodded my head at him, unable to talk as I'd just bitten into a piping hot potato.

He took the bowl from the table, leaving the spoon for my next round and told me he would be back in a few moments. While he was out of the room, I started to wonder who Helen was. Was she someone he knew? Or was she his last victim? Either way, I knew I would find out in time. I hoped my vivid imagination was just conjuring up a scary horror story and I wasn't about to be the main character in one. At least I had a bit of food in my system, so it gave me a bit more of a fighting edge, and I was sure I was going to need it. That became my new plan; to eat and gain back as much energy as possible, because I had a feeling I was going to need it. I had to keep my wits about me.

    I was still angry at Jason for double crossing me, I was annoyed that I allowed him to convinced me he was going to help me escape, only to find out his grand plan was to sell me off to a private buyer. I wondered how much money he got for me. He was clever though, the crazy doctor ordered him to kill me off and instead of doing his job, Jason obviously saw a way he could make a quick few quid. I was stupid and naive enough to believe anyone was going to save me.

    The middle-aged man might have been a bit creepy, but I was telling myself, that he was harmless, although it was obvious that the man was not all there in the head.

    I was preoccupied with my thoughts that I didn't hear the door opening again, and like magic, he was stood in front of me with a fresh bowl of stew.

    I stood up from the table to grab my bowl from his hands, but a look of panic took over his face and he snapped at me to sit back down. The bowl was slammed on the table in front of me and he snarled at me.

    "You do not move unless I give you permission. Do you hear me?" he shouted before rushing over to the door, and slamming it shut.

    I heard him grunting some incoherent words before he returned to the table and sat down opposite me. Anger had taken over his face, his eyes looked glazed over and his pupils were dilated. I wanted to speak, but the look on his face had me recoiling inside. I'd seen that look before; it was the same type of look my father had on his face, moments before an explosive episode. I didn't want to push the man and it didn't help that I still had no real idea of what was expected of me. I knew more than anything, I needed food in my body and a good night's sleep without being drugged up, so I remained silent as I picked up my spoon again to continue eating my meal.

My new captor picked at his fingernails and repeatedly tapped his foot on the concrete floor, clearly something was going on in his mind. His angered expression started to take on a look of worry as he fidgeted in front of me. Being shouted at by him, I could handle but I wasn't expecting the tears again. That I didn't know how to deal with and wondered if I should have offered him a hug, but I still didn't know anything about him and I feared that he was expecting a lot more than I could offer. I didn't want a hug him, but I wanted the crying to stop.

"Can I ask you something?" I spoke with a reluctance in my voice, attempting to cut through the atmosphere.

"You may." He sat forward and placed his hands like a steeple, looking at me over his fingertips. "I may even answer you." He smirked, his voice was smarmy and arrogant.

The weirdo had gone from a sad, upset man to someone resembling a psychopath within seconds. He was like multiple people in one body, and I'd only known him half an hour. It was his cold and nasty stare that had me on edge the most, that and his crying.

I cleared my throat and reached for the plastic cup of water off the table in front of me. Composing my mind and drinking slowly to give me a few more moments to breath. I was becoming too scared to talk but I fought my inner voice. I finished drinking my water, before clearing my throat again.

"Why am I here?" I asked.

"Why wouldn't you be, this is your home."

Why did he keep saying that? It was annoying me, and I couldn't help but show it.

"This isn't my home." I snapped at him.

He stood up from the table and I automatically flinched. I thought he was about to swipe me for raising my voice, but he didn't.

"I do not know why you keep saying that Helen, you were gone for a long time, but surly you remember."

"Remember what, you weirdo."

He slammed his fist on the table, making me jump and almost knocking over what was left of my water. Maybe calling him a weirdo wasn't the best thing I could have done, but the man was deranged if he thought that time warped bedroom was my home.

"Did you buy me?" I asked but he looked at me blankly. "From Jason, did you buy me?" I snapped, I couldn't help it, my frustration was boiling over the surface, and I couldn't hide it.

The man lifted his hand up towards my face and I was sure he was going to hit me but instead his hand cupped my cheek, and he wiped away the single a tear that was trickling down the side of my face.

Affection was unknown to me, I couldn't remembered a time I had ever received an ounce sympathy, never mind someone wiping a tear from my face. I was confused, really confused, and felt uncomfortable at his close proximity. The man was a loose cannon, that much he made obvious, and it scared the living daylights out of me.

"I think it is time for you to go to bed now." He looked me in the eyes, with a mixture of authority and maybe a small glint of sympathy.

Part of me wanted to argue that I wasn't ready for bed, but the other part of me knew that my poor body needed rest more than anything. I was hoping for a goodnights sleep, and guessed I'd sleep better in my little bedsit, than I would have still being held captive at the hospital. I placed my spoon in the table beside my empty bowl and nodded my head in agreement. He then took me by the hand and led me towards the bed like I was a small child. I was half expecting a bedtime story but instead he watched me as I placed my legs under the itchy, scratchy blanket and laid my head down on the pillow. I had to move

my ribcage around one of the springs in the mattress, but it was still more comfortable than the yoga mat I'd been forced to sleep on before.
In that moment I was grateful, and thanked the man. After all, he could have had me sleeping on the floor.

He advised me to get some rest, but then he worried me when he said I had to leave my leg outside the blanket. I went to ask him why but before I had time to speak, he had a tight hold of my ankle, and he was attempting to chain my foot up to the end of the bed. I tried to tell him there was no need and promised him I would be good, but he wouldn't listen, so I kicked out in anger, hoping it would force him to release his grip on me. That didn't happen, I was still feeling weak, and I didn't have enough energy to fight him off.

"Please you do not have to do this." I begged, but he tried to tell me it was for my own good.

"We don't want you wondering off again."

I tried to speak but he covered my mouth with his large hand and warned me to stop trying to fight him, because I wasn't going to win.
The man then tried to convince me that he was only trying to help me, but I was petrified and scared of what he was about to do next. At least in the hospital, the guards had rules and they all feared their psychotic boss. There were people there to make sure the rules were followed. It dawned on me that I was on my own with the middle-aged man and that he could have done anything to me, and nobody would have been any the wiser.

The doctor already thought I was dead, and my parents no doubt believed the same so would it have really mattered if I were murdered. Maybe he wanted to torture me instead? That scared me more than death itself. *I guess when you buy yourself a girl, you can do what the hell you wanted with them.*

"Please." I whimpered but he just stared at me blankly. He smiled his creepy smile, and it sent a shiver down my spine.

"Now sleep, you've a busy day ahead of you tomorrow. Goodnight Helen, I love you."

I had no time to respond to him before the room fell into complete darkness. He'd turned the light off and walked out of the room. I heard the door close, followed by the sound of the locks.

I sat myself up on the bed and reached down to have a feel of my ankle, I was hoping that the man had accidently left me enough space to free myself from the new, upgraded chain holding me in place, but it was no use.

Yet again I was chained up like a mistreated, unloved animal. It didn't help that I hadn't bathed or showered in months, so I was starting to smell like an animal too.

CHAPTER NINE – Four months later

Six months pregnant and he still didn't acknowledge that I was going to be having a baby at some point in the near future, my belly was growing by the day, but I just got dismissed if I ever tried to say anything about the pregnancy. It was like he thought talking about it would make it more real or something, the amount the baby moved about inside my womb, made it obvious to me just how real it all was, and time was counting down.

  Living with them was hard enough, without having a tiny baby to look after as well. I often wondered what life with a baby was going to look like and it filled me with fear and excitement all at the same time. Darren, with his creepy smile and schizophrenic tenancies was still the nice one out of the two men, his son Martin not so much. Martin could be a little twisted at times and I was sure he liked playing mind games with me. He would try and convince me I had said something, or forgotten to do one of my chores, even though I knew otherwise. I had a feeling he was trying to get me in trouble with his dad, Darren because he was jealous of me. How anyone could be jealous of a live in slave was beyond me, but it was definitely the case. Martin had his dad all to himself, until I showed up.

  I had gotten used to being called Helen by that point although I never did get to the bottom of why he called me that name, and his son reckoned he didn't know the reason either, which I knew was a bare cheek lie because he'd always smirk at me behind his dad's back any time the name was mentioned, but it was what it was, just another one of Martin's petty mind games. The men weren't as hard on me as they were when I first arrived in my new prison, mainly because they both realised I wasn't planning on running away and in all honestly, I had gotten used to our weird little set up. The thought of escaping crossed my mind from time to time, but I realised quickly enough that I had nowhere to go, not being a six-month pregnant girl anyway.

Could you imagine if I had returned home to my parents? I had on plenty of occasions and no matter how positive I wanted me to be, I couldn't see an outcome which was good for either, me or my baby.

To top it all off, carrying a baby meant I had zero energy most days and I was getting too fat to run anywhere. I knew I was probably in the best place, until the baby was born at least. The fear of being homeless, of living on the streets with a newborn was enough to keep me there, and I was fed three times a day. More than what could have been said, living with my father. I was able to wash and keep clean and I was warm, a lot more than what could have been said six months previously.

Twice a week Darren would give me permission to enter the upstairs part of their home, the large metal door which separated the living quarters would be left open on those days, which helped air out my space because being cooped up in the same room for weeks on end, caused a lot of unwelcoming smells. Something my hormonal nose didn't take to kindly to. I often found myself hugging the toilet seat too, at first it was most evenings, but that eased in time and the sickness wasn't as bad during the second trimester. I also enjoyed having that extra room to walk around, it was a weird sense of freedom, even if I was only allowed up the stairs to complete my chores, it was a step in the right direction. My main job was to clean up after them both and do their laundry. I was basically their live-in maid but as a reward, I was allowed to take a nice warm bath once every fortnight. Baths were a luxury, which was something I had always taken for granted in the past. I was allowed to wash my clothes once a week and thankfully the horrific dresses Darren had me in at the start, didn't fit over my baby bump so I was given a long navy t shirt and a pair of Martins shorts. Martin was a big man, so the shorts were a little baggy on me, but I was grateful to have something comfortable to wear and not be in a ridiculous dress. Being pregnant was uncomfortable as it was, without having to squeeze into tight, ghastly clothes.

 It took me weeks of sweet-talking Darren, but I was finally granted permission to cook dinner for them both and they enjoyed my cooking so much that it became one of my new chores. On the odd occasion, I'd have been given permission to eat the same meal as the two men, although sitting at the table and eating as a trio wasn't something that happened too often.

 Nine times out of ten, I would prepare a simple meal, something pretty basic, as my mother never got chance to teach me how to cook.

 Darren taught me how to boil potatoes and steam veg, which was more than I'd ever been taught at home. While I was peeling the veg one of the afternoons, Darren admitted to me, that if it were up to him, he would have had me upstairs eating with them a lot more often, but his son didn't like me, and Martin never tried to hide the fact that he despised me either.

Martin could get really funny with me if he saw my face too often, so Darren would often sneak me upstairs while his son was out on an errand or busy doing something else, outside the property.

During the week, Darren was so happy with my behaviour, I was gifted a colouring book and a small pack of crayons, which I thought was a little childish at first, but I soon appreciated my time to colour in and not having to worry about anything else. Martin teased me about it, saying I was acting like a four-year-old child, not almost fourteen years old, but I didn't care what he said. At the end of the day, it was something just for me and Martin hated that.

I loved having my own thing to do and for the majority of the evening, I had no chores to complete as the housework was always finished nice and early in the morning, just in case anyone turned up unannounced. No one ever did turn up, but Darren was a paranoid man. I suppose kidnapping a teenage girl and keeping her captive in your basement would do that to you. I found myself having a lot of time on my own with not much to do so colouring became my hobby. I also spent a lot of time talking to my stomach, hopeful that the baby could hear me, so I didn't feel so lonely. That baby heard all my hopes and fears, but mainly my hopes and dreams because I didn't want to corrupt the child before it was even born. I often wondered what they were going to look like, whether they would look like me or John, I hoped myself because John wasn't ugly, but he wasn't a pretty boy either. I couldn't wait to find out the sex of the baby either and found it hard to think of names for either sex. I wondered if other mothers had the same problem. *How do you name a baby?*

I'd been living with Darren and Martin for just under five months and as much as I knew the whole situation was messed up and wrong on so many levels, I did wonder if it was any worse than still living at home with my father and his outrageous rules and regulations. As least Darren didn't use physical violence on me. His son however was a little more unpredictable and had given me a back hander on a few occasions but that was usually because I'd become a little too cocky, or it was down to jealously because his dad was spending more time with me, than him. Martin was in his early twenties, but he would act a lot younger when he started to kick off. I did wonder about the man's mental state, neither of the men where one hundred percent right in the head, they couldn't have been. One minute Martin could be nice and calm, and within seconds he would be trashing the place, shouting abuse, and being rather threatening to both me and his father. His outbursts would cause a horrible atmosphere between us all and I think Darren was a little fearful of his son, not that he'd have ever admitted that, but it was obvious to me at least.

My father was just as unpredictable and because of that, I believed that gave me an edge, I thought I could somehow calm Martin down, but that didn't end well for me.

Martin and his dad argued for two days straight after I tried to help calm him down once. I was rewarded with a slap across the face, so hard I landed on my arse on the floor. That was the only time I knew Darren had acknowledged my pregnancy as he argued with his son and ordered him out of the house for the rest of the day. I was okay and Darren having my back made me feel slightly protected by him, at least where his son was concerned.

I often lay in that springy bed at night and wondered if I was ever missed, like did my parents try and look for me? or maybe my old mates wondered where I could have gone. I bet they all assume I was dead. All those questions and more, occupied the space in my mind for a good hour before I would fall to sleep at night, the rest of the time I spent talking to my unborn baby, and getting to understand their little routine while they grew inside me. The baby seemed to want to play kick about as soon as I would lay down, maybe because they had more room to move about, but it did make drifting off to sleep a little harder at times, which meant my mind had plenty of time to wonder. With that in mind, I had been trying my damn hardest not let the whole situation stress me out, because the days I'd been an emotional wreck, were the days my pregnancy would take it out of me. I was sure that stress wasn't good for the baby either.

***

Darren realised within a few weeks of me being with them that I didn't need to be chained to my bed every single night. It was more hassle than it was worth when I woke one morning in desperate need of a pee, and wasn't able to move. Darren was angry with me at first and ordered I washed my own bedsheets by hand before I was allowed any food or drink that day but after calming down he realised it was beyond my control. I made a promise that I could be trusted, and from that day I was no longer bound to my bed.

It wasn't as if I could escape anyway, there was a big metal door in my way and a whole house that resembled Fort Knox to escape. It was evident to everyone, including me, that I was going nowhere. Like I said before, I had nowhere to run to anyway, because there was no way I would have returned back home to my vile father, I'm sure he would have loved having a pregnant teenage daughter back home to bully.

I actually felt more at ease and relaxed in captivity, than I ever felt in my own family home.

How messed up is that?

I was starting to actually feel okay about everything, living with the two men wasn't all that bad and if anything, I was looking forward to us having a baby in the house. I was hoping having a cute little baby around the place would be enough to break the icy exterior of Martin and I had a feeling Darren was good with children at one point. After all he raised his son on his own for the best part of his childhood when his wife died of cancer, Martin was only six years old and never remembered his mother. At first I thought that was who Helen was, but Martin reckoned his dad didn't know anyone by that name. A bit bloody weird that he took to notion to call me that, and it was frustrating me not knowing why. Martin knew more than he was letting on, but got extremely aggressive with me, anytime I tried to bring the subject up. Darren would just shake his head at me and walk away, which gave his son time to bully me, so it was easier not knowing, even if I hated not knowing all of the facts.

***

I woke one morning to an almighty bang on the ceiling above me, it made me jump out of my skin. It was still dark outside, so it had to be the early hours. Something was clearly happening upstairs above me, there was a lot of moving and dragging of furniture which seemed very odd for that time of the morning. Maybe the men were having a change around. *Great that can only mean more housework for me*, I thought to myself. I didn't mind cleaning, if anything I found it passed the time of day, but my pregnant stomach was starting to weigh me down, literally. I sat myself up in bed and listened intently. I heard voices, voices I didn't recognise. Both a male voice and a one of a female. I tried my hardest to make out the words, but the basement was almost soundproof so all I could make out were the different tones in their voices. Darren and Martin had never had visitors in the five months I'd been there, although they were always paranoid about people turning up unannounced so the curtains would remain closed. The sound of visitors had me feeling a small ping of fear and wishful thinking, all at the same time. I had often wondered what it would have been like to be rescued, wondering what trouble Martin and Darren would be in if they were ever caught.

Then fear took over again as I worried that the female voice could belong to the psychotic doctor and one males could be of her minions. *Had she come back to get me after finding out I was alive?* Surely not, surely she would just be glad to see the back of me, or maybe she was scared I knew too much. I also wondered about Leanne and whether or not she was still at the hellhole or whether she'd already been sold on, and don't get me started Jenny, I would've loved to know why she acted like she'd been abducted, why she lied to us and what her and her horrid mother were up to. I bet the crazy doctor was continuing her manipulating web of sex trafficking, but I had hoped she'd been caught. I couldn't understand how she could get away with stealing girls and selling them on, how did no one ever flag her up? The hospital hellhole I was held in was a big building, surely someone would have suspected something. Unless it was part of a massive coverup, you hear shit like that in books and stuff. Governments covering up mass murders, maybe the hospital was one of those coverups. It made more sense, that anything else I thought up.

It was only when I thought about all those other girls, that I'd fantasise about escaping and reporting the doctor and her minions to the police, but who would believe a fourteen-year-old pregnant teenager, over a rich, powerful psycho bitch of a doctor? I know who I'd believe, and it wouldn't have been a teenage mother to be, that was for sure.

The voices above me were raised, but I still couldn't make out any words, then all of a sudden, it went deadly quiet. A weird silence that had me feeling scared and on high alert. That silence lasted for most of the day. Something really strange was happening and Darren had his routines, so it really wasn't like him. I would usually have had the whole house cleaned by the time the postman arrived, but no one had been down to see me, and I assumed both men were out of the house for the day. Whoever the strangers were, it sounded like Darren and Martin both left with them which didn't seem right to me.

By the early evening I was starting to get hunger pains, but I felt sick at the same time and my baby was doing somersaults inside me, which wasn't helping. Without my routine, I had no idea of the time of day it was and after sitting around for what seemed like the entire day, I curled myself up on the bed, and attempted to sleep my sicky feeling away.

I'd been starved in the pass, but I couldn't afford not to eat with an unborn child desperately needing the subsistence just as much as I did.

CHAPTER TEN – Then there were two

It was the middle of the night before I heard any sounds again, muffled footsteps above me and the slam of the front door an indication they were both home. I had no idea where they had been for the entire day, but guessed I would find out soon enough, so I let myself drift back off to sleep. Only to be startled awake a few hours later with Darren stood over me. I must have been exhausted because I would have normally heard them coming down the stairs, but I heard nothing. I jumped out of my skin and pulled myself up to sit up in bed. I was instantly worried because he looked angry, and Darren rarely looked angry those days, so something had clearly pissed him off.

"Morning Darren, I didn't hear you come in." I said, a little reluctance in my voice as I didn't know what to expect.

"He's gone." Darren announced but I was unsure on what he meant, until I saw a tear dripping down the man's face.

"What do you mean?" I asked getting to my feet.

"I mean he is gone!"

He paused and was about to walk away from me. "I don't even know what to do with you now. This was never the plan."

"Darren, I do not know what you are talking about, what do you mean he is gone?" I asked.

"He is gone, my boy is gone, and it is all your fault!" Darren spat his words at me.

He turned on his heels and walked towards me again, scowling at me to get dressed and be quick about it. I was confused but also scared and started grabbing my clothes ready to get changed when he started crying. I didn't know what to do, what to say so I placed my arms around his shoulders and tried to comfort him. I hadn't ever comforted a man before and it felt awkward as hell, but it seemed like the right thing to do at the time.

"What happened Darren? Speak to me please." I tried to talk gently, "talk to me please."

"He didn't listen to me," Darren sobbed into my shoulder, "if he'd just listened, then the argument wouldn't have gotten so out of hand. Why didn't he listen?"

I felt like he was confessing something, but what, I didn't know. I couldn't understand what he was getting at.

"Where is Martin?" I asked but I was rewarded with a look of horror and a backhander to the side of my cheek. I took a step back, covering the hot, stinging sensation taking over the side of my face and looked at Darren, shaking my head. Striking me was never his thing, Darren had other ways of punishing me, so I was stunned.

"We were arguing over you!" He said coldly, then he stared directly at me, he looked me deep in the eyes. "You and that fucking baby growing inside you." He hissed at me, "Martin wanted rid of you, said you are too much hassle, but I said no, and he went behind my back. He stabbed me in the back Helen, his own father." Tears were dripping down the sides of his face.

I didn't speak, I didn't feel it was the right time to reply, instead I just looked at him, and for a split second I witnessed a real vulnerability to his character, I found myself feeling sorry for him.

"He wanted me to get rid of you and that baby, but I told him I couldn't, he didn't understand. Maybe I should have listened to him, my son would be still here, if you were out of the picture."

I had never felt wanted, never knew what love was but Darren's words in that moment cut me deep. I actually believed he liked me but the way he was talking to me in that situation proved to me, I was still as unwanted as ever.

"I know you are hurting, but please don't say that. I am here for you Darren." I tried to comfort him, but he raised his hand up like he was about to swipe me again and I automatically flinched out of the way.

He stopped himself, you could tell he was thinking about his actions and thought best of it, then he lifted his finger up as if he was about to speak, but instead he turned on his feet and made his way out of my room. he stopped when he got to the doorway and smirked at me.

"You don't know shit, you little whore." He scowled before slamming my door closed and locking it behind him.

I had never know Darren to talk to me with such a vicious tongue and I was upset. I'm sure the pregnancy hormones didn't help, but I spent the rest of that evening, crying. Part of me upset because of my situation. Upset because of the way Darren was treating me and upset for him, the man who had just lost his only child.

***

The dust had settled a little and a few days later, Darren sat me down and explained the events that led to his son's death. The male and female voices I had heard in the middle of the night were a couple who were under the impression that I was selling them my baby.
Martin had it all figured out and went behind his father's back, trying to make out I wanted to put my child up for adoption because I was a scared teenager girl, who wasn't ready to be a mum.

That may have been slightly true but the thought of giving my baby up for adoption had never crossed my mind.

Darren was a nice and gentle man usually, admittedly not all there in the head, but Darren felt like his son was hell bend on trying to ruin everything. To make matters worse his selfish actions had only gone and shone a spotlight on the family, two single men advertising a woman as a surrogate mother in the local shop, was a foolish move. Martin admitted it was a gamble but said he didn't care whether his dad got caught or not. Martin believed his father was far too soft on me and he hated the attention I got, even if it was minimal.

Darren treated me with respect most of the time and I almost felt like he'd been forced into being obnoxious towards me at times because of he didn't, his bully of a son would have been a bit more forceful and nasty towards me. I had a mouth on me at the start, but I had calmed down a lot during my time in captivity. I know it was stupid but wanted to believe that Darren actually cared for my wellbeing, unlike his jealous son who always treated me like I was a nothing but a nuisance. It wasn't as if I'd asked to be abducted and sold to his dad, but you would have thought that were the case. I was starting to believe Darren actually enjoyed having me around, but that day changed absolutely everything, and it wasn't my fault for a change.

***

The day of Martin's funeral came, and I wasn't just warned constantly about my noise or trying anything silly, I was also chained to the bed and had a gag placed over my mouth. It didn't matter how many times I'd told Darren I would be silent and promised not to make a fuss, he didn't trust me anymore and told me his family would be visiting and he wasn't going to chance me ruining anything else.

    Being held captive was starting to take its toll on me and my body. It was a struggle, to stay awake, but I also struggled to fall asleep because the baby decided they wanted to use me as a trampoline and hadn't stopped kicking my insides for the best part of an hour.

    My child wasn't even born, but I planned to do everything in my power to keep them safe, a lot safer than I kept myself. I couldn't do much until they were born but I knew the best thing I could do for my baby in that moment was to remain calm. I remembered my mother being pregnant with my little brother, she'd often be stressing out about something or another, which wasn't hard to do, living in our house, but that led to my brother being born two months early. Alex was extremely sick and needed to spend time in hospital as his lungs were underdeveloped. I couldn't chance anything like that happening to my baby and couldn't see me being allowed to attend the hospital if it were ever needed, so I had no choice but to remain calm and just let things be. I couldn't wait to meet my baby, for more reasons than most mothers, I needed them t be born before I could come up with an escape plan. Darren made it abundantly clear, that I was no longer wanted there, and treated me as such.

    I heard the voices above me, raised voices but it sounded like they are having fun, partying as it was Martin's wake. I thought about shaking at the chains in a hope that someone would hear me, but I also knew I was just asking for trouble. I was bored senseless and wanted some entertainment, but I knew it wasn't worth my while. I spent the majority of that day drifting in and out of sleep until later that evening when Darren eventually came down to unchain me. Just in time too, as I was about to pee myself again. I felt like I should have wet the bed just to prove a point, but it was a gruelling day for the man, and I respected that. After seeing his face, the last thing I wanted to do, was add any more stress to the situation.

He looked a bit worse for wear and it was obvious that he'd spent the best part of the evening drinking because the man was swaying on his feet, and slurring incoherent words. I climbed down off the bed and ran straight to the toilet to relive myself. A few bangs came from the other side of the door. I flushed the chain and opened the door I was startled, Darren was stood the other side of the door, his body taking up the space in the doorway, and he was looking pretty menacing.

"You made me jump." I admitted.

"You made me kill my own son." He said, clear as day.

I didn't make the man do anything, and could only assume what happened as Darren hadn't been particularly good at explaining the whole situation, I only knew of the events leading up to his demise.

"I told him." He slurs. "I told him you are part of this family as much as him."

He paused and I could see he had started to shake; it took me a second to realise he was sobbing. I thought about hugging him again, but I didn't feel like it was the right time, he was drunk and no doubt he would have lashed out at me.

Darren walked away from me and sat on the end of my bed, so I made my way over to try and comfort the grieving man with my words. I felt sorry for him. *I know, crazy?* I'd been kidnapped and held captive by him, yet I felt sorry for him because he'd just buried his own child.

I wondered if my own parents had a memorial or anything like that for me, I'd been missing for months by that point, they must have assumed I was dead. Seeing Darren so cut up, had me wondering how my own mother was dealing with everything and I hoped she wasn't too distraught. My father on the other hand I doubted he even shed a tear.

After talking with Darren for almost an hour, I found out that Martin was planning on killing me off once I give birth to the baby, he was trying to convince his father that it was the best possibility for everyone, everyone except me that was. Martin knew he'd messed up by advertising a pregnant woman in their home and decided killing me once I gave birth was the sensible thing to do, but Darren was a lot of things, a murder wasn't one of them. Part of me was thankful that Darren defended me but that turned into a father and son scrap, and evidently caused Martin to fall and whack his head off the granite mantel piece. It was clear that the whole thing was an accident, but Darren watched on as his son bled out. Instead of ringing for an ambulance or shouting for help, his dad calmly sat on the edge sofa and watched until his son took his last breath.

I believe Darren was in shock. Martin had threatened his father that if he didn't kill me off, he was going to report him to the police himself. He then tried to threaten Darren with horror stories about what they would do to man who kidnapped young girls. Martin told his father that he'd rather his dad was behind bars, than living a fucked up lie and pretending I was his long-lost daughter or something. Either way, Darren couldn't see a way out of the situation with his son in the picture, so he left him there, lying motionless on the floor. Knowing that Darren was trying to protect me, had me feeling a weird sense of happiness that someone finally had my best interests at heart, I hadn't felt that since I was a little kid, staying with my grandmother.

Living in the house with Darren became no better than the home I was raised in, and I knew I needed more than that for my baby, but I was trapped. Held captive and due to give birth within the month. My fantasy about living with the men as a family once the baby was born was shattered and I knew that it was never going to be the same again. It wasn't just Martin that was dead, but my dreams of a peaceful life were gone with him.

***

It took a good while before Darren could look at me like I hadn't caused his son's death, but he did eventually start treating me like I was a member of his family again and he finally acknowledged that we'd soon have a baby sharing his home.

CHAPTER ELEVEN – A little taste of freedom

As the weeks passed, life at Darren's had improved dramatically, no longer was I locked in the basement for the best part of the day, I had a lot more freedom. The only time the door was bolted, was if Darren had to go out, or at bedtime. As long as Darren was at home, which was most of the time, I was allowed to walk freely between both dwellings. The only rule I was given, was to stay away from the windows and doors, which was easy when the curtains where always drawn closed. The front porch led out to a hallway which was always locked, with a multitude of padlocks, but the back door was my biggest test. A large wooden door with leaded glass panels looking out onto open fields, complete with mature trees, way in out the distance.

That was real freedom, and it was just out of reach. I'd been caught a few times standing too close to the back door, and been rewarded with a swipe to the back of the head, a reminder of my boundaries. The first time I was caught, Darren went crazy at me, and I was locked back downstairs as a punishment, but apart from staying away from the windows and doors, I had more freedom than I ever did in my life. I felt like I was a member of the house, not a prisoner and I think Darren enjoyed the company too.

It was my fourteen birthday when Darren got me my own TV after allowing me to watch the odd movie upstairs with him. He told me he would be in charge of how often I could watch it, but it was ultimately for me and my baby.

Darren still had his moments where he'd be in a foul mood, but the man was still grieving, and the fireplace was a constant reminder to the both of us of what took place in that room only a few weeks before. I had scrubbed the mantel piece for days on end in an attempt to get the blood stains out of the wooden surround, but it had seeped into the old wood too much and it took a lot of attempts before it was no longer visible.

Darren often talked about Martin as a child, and how loving and kind he was. Apparently he was a loving little boy who went out of his way to help others. That didn't sound like the Martin I had known but I took his father's word for it. Darren told me that up until Martin hit his adult years, he was an affectionate and supportive type of son. Darren said it all changed when Martin made friends with Anoushka, the woman I knew as the psychotic doctor from the compound. Martin got involved with the woman when he was eighteen and he was madly in love with her which made it easy for him to be groomed himself. Martin ended up helping the woman, groom young girls because he believed Anoushka was in love with him too, and helping her was his way of being able to prove his love towards her. She played Martin good and proper, and it left him nasty and twisted. Darren never found out what it was, but he knew Anoushka had a hold over his son and still did until his dying day. I finally understood why I was there in the first place and how Darren was involved in it all. It took Martin to be out of the picture before I found out why I was being called Helen for so long.

Darren had two children originally, Martin, and his younger sister Helen, who went missing at the age of ten. Martin refused to speak about his baby sister, which was weird, and it wouldn't have surprised me if the psychotic Russian doctor had something to do with Helen's disappearance. Maybe she was Anoushka's first ever abduction, she was only nineteen when she first lured a girl home from a pub, only to help a group of men abduct her. No one knew what Anoushka had against young girls, but clearly something happened to make her so twisted.

Martin met Anoushka a year later, she was twenty, while Martin had just turned eighteen but within months of the two of them meeting, poor Helen went missing while out playing at the local park.

I had seen photos of Helen and could see why Darren could have mistaken me for her at the very start, she had the same mousey coloured hair as me and blue eyes, although we still looked quite different there were similarities.

I'd tried to press Darren for more information about the compound, the place where myself and the girls were held captive, but he didn't give much away. Either he was just as in the dark as I was, or he did know more than he let on and just didn't trust me enough to open up. He was learning to trust me though, and every day gave me new information, I just needed to listen closely to his drunken rabbling in the evenings. Clues would be in the way he worded things, or in his body language. Knowing any of it wasn't much use to me still being held captive and it wasn't as if Darren was ever going to let me just walk out of the door. He knew himself, too much had happened for him to ever let me go free and if he was going to gain any morals, it would have already happened. Darren didn't believe he was ever doing anything wrong, and that included keeping me locked up away from the rest of the world. It was during one of the evening while Darren was drinking, when I found out I was sold for twenty-five thousand pounds, half price for the going child, because I was with child myself. It was a shock to find out fifty grand was the going rate for a teenage girl, knowing that made me sick and also made me realise I could have been sold off a hell of a long time ago, had my father known I'd have fetched such a decent price.

***

Over the following weeks, I found that I was spending more time upstairs, and a lot less time on my own. Darren was worried that the baby would be making an appearance sooner, rather than later and he'd mentioned how the dynamics of the house would need to change to accommodate the new baby.

"Means we will get less quality time together, just the two of us." Darren said, sounding a little disappointed.

"I am sure I will still find time to look after you too Darren."

"I look forward to it." He smiled at me but there was something about his look which had me overthinking for most of that night.

CHAPTER TWELVE – A little bundle of Hope

I had never been so scared in my life as I was the day my baby decided they were making an appearance. I was thirty-six weeks pregnant and in the middle of cooking dinner for Darren and myself when my waters broke. It was a sunny afternoon, as the blazing sun was beating through the curtains, making the place very stuffy, and the air thicker than normal. It wouldn't have killed Darren to jar open a window, but he didn't trust I wouldn't try and sneak out and run away. I couldn't have ran anyway, my big belly wouldn't have fit through the windows, but Darren believed I was just saying that to him, to trick him into placing his trust in me. He was being ridiculous but there were little point in telling him, once Darren got something into his head, nobody would be able to convince him otherwise. A stubborn Leo man with a massive chip on his shoulder.

    It was around four o'clock during the day when I started getting aches in my lower stomach. At first I believed it was the baby just kicking about, so I tried to power on through it because dinner was almost ready, and I was starving. I was cooking pork chops that evening with apple sauce, one of Darren's favourite meals.

"Are you okay?" he asked seeing me clearly in pain.

"I'm fine." I said but I wasn't fine at all, my contractions had started, mildly at first until my waters broke and created a puddle on the kitchen floor between my legs.

I had thought about that day for months, but it finally happening scared me. I started to cry, uncontrollable tears. Thankfully, Darren knew what to do and ordered me to go downstairs and lay down on my bed. My shorts were soaked through, so he told me to try and relax while he fetched me some towels. I was scared, and in more pain than I expected but I wasn't about to allow myself to be defeated. I was about to give birth and I'm not sure the realisation really hit me until that point when my labour began.

Within minutes I was having stronger contractions, but they were spaced apart. Even so, it felt like I had just gained my breath back, and it was being taken away again in an instant.

I lay on that bed, panting and begging for it all to be over for almost two hours before I felt the urgent need to push. The burning pain as my babies head appeared was enough to make me pass out but Darren shock me back to life, just in time for my final push. I was in and out of it, but he kept talking to me and reassuring me that I was doing brilliantly, and it would all be over soon. I needed those encouraging words in that moment.

I was very weak but managed to do what I needed to do, and my baby girl was laid in between my legs, screaming her little lungs off. Darren went out of the room and returned with a massive pair of scissors.

"Please, I am begging you. Don't hurt her please." I begged convinced he was going to do as Martin had threatened and kill me off as soon as she was born.

He'd tricked me, maybe he wanted to sell the baby after all.

"Calm down!" Darren shouted at me, "it is to cut the cord."

"The, what?" I asked.

"The babies umbilical cord."

I felt stupid as it was, and it didn't help that Darren was smirking at me. He told me I had a lot to learn and placed my daughter on my chest while he helped to clean up the bloody mess between my legs. He then made me feel sick when he said he needed to pull the placenta out of me. I didn't even know what a placenta was, but he explained it tome as best as he could and all I could do was take his word for it. The man seemed to know a lot more about childbirth than I did, and I was too much in my own world to argue, I was mesmerised staring down at my baby that to be honest the man could have done anything to me, and I doubt I'd have noticed.

I had no energy to disagree with him anyway and my newborn had started to scream in my face which scared me a little because I had no idea what I was supposed to do next. I hadn't really thought that far ahead, which seemed foolish at the time, but I was only fourteen years old and never had a baby before, so everything was brand new to me.

"Put the baby on you breast, it's hungry." Darren explained before pulling my insides out of me.

I automatically threw up all over the floor, mainly tea because I hadn't eaten much and for a minute I wondered if he'd caused me even more damage as I felt the blood seeping from my insides. *Was he certain my placenta needed to be removed?* I had never heard of it before, so I was apprehensive to say the least. *Maybe that was his way of killing me off, and I'd just allowed him to do it.* My mind was on overdrive.

I already felt embarrassed, and my baby was crying because she'd just been accidently swished against my pillow. Darren helped clean up the mess I'd created on the floor and then he passed me a towel to clean up myself.

I was pretty grateful to Darren because he was supportive towards me and the baby in that first hour. I would have been completely useless without him there.

My tiny daughter latched herself onto my boob like she knew exactly what to do, which was more than I could say about myself. I assumed I would just naturally know, but the labour had messed with my brain, and I was feeling extra emotional.

I lay down on my side, watching on as my baby girl suckled on me, she was so peaceful and content.

Her perfect little, tiny fingers wrapped around my own and for a second I forgot where we both were. Darren left the room after checking I was okay and advised me to get some rest, while he went and cleaned up the mess I'd left him in the kitchen. I was half expecting to be sent upstairs to clean it myself, but I wasn't to know my waters were going to break. I guessed he was going to turn the light off which was an indication that it was time for bed, but fifteen minutes later, he returned with my diced pork chops, mashed potato, and mushy peas.

"I guessed you'd need food after that ordeal." He said smiling at me, "I'm proud of you, y'know."

Darren rarely praised me, and it felt nice. I thanks him for my food, and I was starving. I lay my newborn baby on my pillow as I sat myself up in bed to devour my dinner.

The next morning Darren offered to babysit my daughter while I took a well needed bath. After childbirth and really needed to freshen up, but I didn't trust him with her and told him I wanted to keep her with me. He thought I was being stupid, but I just didn't feel safe leaving my helpless child in his care, especially with the threat his son had mentioned still rattling around in my brain. Yes, it was true, Darren was the nicest of the two men, but at the end of the day, he was the one who paid for me in the first place. He knew I was pregnant and even if he wasn't planning on hurting me, I couldn't help but wonder how much he'd fetch for a perfect newborn girl. *More than fifty grand?* I never fully trusted him, but any faith I did have in him, was ruined the day his son died.

Darren tried to argue with me, saying the bathroom wasn't safe for a newborn baby but as clueless as I was, I didn't see the harm in her being in the same room as me while I bathed. I had vowed to never let her out of my sight, and the baby needed my protection. That's what I believed a mother should be. The protector.

Pity the same couldn't have been said about my own mother. She would have loved having a granddaughter around the house, I was sure of it. My father on the other hand wouldn't have allowed it. Had I never had been abducted, I doubt I would have been allowed to go through with the pregnancy. I would have brought shame on the family. That made me realise I could never return to my parents' home, and they wouldn't get chance to meet my baby, they didn't deserve to be part of either of our lives.

Not that I had much choice in the matter, but it felt like I had some control at least.

Eventually Darren let me have my own way, but as usual the door was to remain unlocked, which I agreed to. One thing with Darren was, he respected my privacy most of the time.

I lay in the warm bath water, splashing my feet gently while watching her sleeping peacefully. Plenty of times over the months leading up to her birth, I'd contemplated ending my life, believing it was easier than dealing with all of the abuse I was being subjected to, but every time I got into those dark thoughts, I brought myself back with thoughts of my baby. I didn't realise I would love a little person so much and that love was enough to stop me doing anything stupid, even before meeting her. She became my reason for living, and the reason neither of us could stay with Darren anymore, my baby deserved batter. That tiny girl gave me an inner strength I didn't know I had and because of that, I decided to name her Hope, Hope Everdeen.

When I returned from my bath, Darren looked angry, and I made the mistake of asking him what was wrong. He didn't answer my question, instead I was ordered to stay in my room and told he was locking the door because he didn't want to hear my baby cry. She wasn't a teary baby and apart from a little whimper when she needed changed or wanted a feed, she was pretty easy to look after. Darren was clearly pissed off because I didn't hide the fact that I didn't trust him with Hope.

I was proud of myself because I felt like I was taking to motherhood like a duck on water. Helping my mother with my siblings growing up gave me a little bit of experience.

I was sat on my bed, baby in my arms and I watched as the door to the basement was closed behind us. I heard the clinking of the locks and I smiled to myself. I couldn't have cared less if we were locked up anymore because for the first time in a long time, I wasn't alone. I had my daughter with me, my very own little family and Darren wasn't part of that, which suited me down to the ground.

CHAPTER THIRTEEN – Eight months later

Hope was a dream to look after, she rarely gave me any trouble at all, but Darren on the other hand had become jealous of mine and my daughters natural bond. I could see where he son got it from. At first I thought it was just a phase when she was first born, but his behaviour became more and more erratic as time went on. He started becoming very heavy handed with me and just as twisted as his deceased son had been.

I was locked back downstairs, and he told me he didn't trust me helping him around the house anymore as he didn't trust I wouldn't poison him. I can't deny the thought hadn't crossed my mind but doing something like that was harder than you'd imagine. It also meant a lot less chores for me, so it was win, win really.

My biggest issue was Darren had started not only threatening me but also threatening my daughter if I didn't give into his every demand, which included having sex with the dirty old man when he'd had too much to drink. I had no choice in the matter so I would just lie there and attempt to block him out until he'd finished which never took longer than twenty minutes and half the time he was too drunk to even know what he was doing. With rape being added to my list of punishments, I had to protect my daughter from seeing the abuse I was being subjected to. The best way I could do that, was every time Darren entered my room, I'd make sure Hope was out of sight.

To start off with, she was small enough fit in the bottom drawer of my wardrobe, but she grew out of it within the space of weeks. I then placed what little clothes we both owned into my rucksack and made her a bed in the bottom of the wardrobe; it became her little hideaway, and we turned it into a game in the end. The rucksack was always packed ready just in case there was ever an opportunity to make a run for it, not that I was going to waste my time on holding my breath for that outcome, being locked away again meant it was very unlikely and just like my mother, I finally accepted that this was the way I was meant to live my life. At least I was still alive.

How my daughter didn't cry when Darren was in the room with us was beyond me, but I should have known she'd be well behaved because she usually was. I'm not sure I could have dealt with a crying child while I was having to deal with Darren.

My main meals had gone back to sandwiches, and it was obvious that Darren wasn't cooking for himself either, as he often made reference to me needing to cook his dinner, but that would mean me leaving my dungeon, and he wasn't about to let that happen any time soon.

He'd started drinking heavily again; it was obvious from the loud music and banging throughout the evenings. Sometimes it was so loud neither me or Hope could sleep until he'd finally passed out himself.

Darren still never had any visitors, but I'd hear him spend a lot of the time talking and singing away to himself. I could usually escape the night without any unwanted attention as long as Hope was settled.

***

It was a Sunday evening; I knew this as I should have celebrated my birthday, so I was down anyway. Hope had developed a rash and was feverish, she never cried like she did that evening, and it didn't matter what I tried to do, I couldn't seem to settle her. I swaddled my daughter like I did when she was a newborn and sang quietly to her, while bouncing gently. It was a routine which worked with her all the time, but not that night.

"Please Hope, time to settle." She wiggled in my arms clearly she didn't like being rocked but I didn't know what else to do.

She'd been fed from my boob, bathed in a cool bath to lower her temperature, and had a fresh nappy on and light weight clothes, I was all out of ideas. I knew I needed to talk to Darren and ask him for some soft foods when he planned my next shop, because at eight months of age, Hope was getting hungrier by the day and my breast were sore from feeding her. By eight months old Hope already had a tooth through and was cutting even more. I was starting to feel like my nipples were going to dry up and fall off. And her biting down on me, was painful.

What didn't help was I hated asking that man for anything, especially things I needed for my daughter. For a while I think he'd forget I was a mother, so any mention of Hope, had me recoiling inside, fearing what my request would cost me dearly.

A loud thudding above me was an indication that Darren had heard Hope's cries, and my heart started racing as I heard his footsteps above me.

"Shush, baby, please."

The footsteps above us stopped just as Hope calmed down, and I sighed a breath of relief, I hoped Darren was too drunk to move because I hadn't the energy to try and keep him entertained, nor did I have the energy to fight him off if he turned on me again. The last time I ended up having a black eye and split lip because he was forcing me to perform oral sex on him and apparently I wasn't trying hard enough, he said could tell I was resisting. The sick twat told me I needed to convince him I was enjoying myself, otherwise I would suffer the consequences. I hated every millisecond of that punishment, but I would act less repelled by the man, just to keep his mood in check.

My wishful thinking didn't last long as I heard the footsteps above us once again, then the dreaded sound of his heeled boots on the wooden staircase leading down to my door. Hope was still whimpering but I rushed over to the wardrobe and placed her in the makeshift basket. I'd just closed the wardrobe door shut as Darren stumbled into my room, clearly pissed up again which wasn't ideal for a recovering alcoholic.

"You've been told… to keep… it silent." He slurred his words, referring to my child.

"I have tried, but she won't settle tonight."

"Then maybe you need me to shut her up."

His tongue would get nastier the more alcohol he'd consumed, and I warned him to leave her the hell alone.

"She is just hungry; my milk isn't enough anymore."

"I am hungry." He says, a horrible grin takes over his face and I know what was coming next.

"She is crying, you cannot expect me to do that now." I said but I should have known that was a mistake.

"I expect you to do as you are told." He shouted.

Hope started crying again but I knew if I opened the wardrobe door, Darren would turn his attention to her. I stared at him, watching his expression, trying to gauge what was about to happen next.

"I couldn't fuck you with that racket anyway." He snapped at me before turning on his unstable feet and wobbling back out of my room.

"She needs baby food." I shouted just as the door closed shut behind him.

"She needs shot." He shouted back at me from the top of the stairs.

It was a few months after giving birth, I saw Darren's true colours, the man would get drunk and force himself onto me, telling me that he loved me, and loving couples where expected to have sex. One minute he thought I was his long-lost daughter, the next, I was his wife. It was the biggest head fuck ever and I felt like I was losing my own mind at times. As soon as I wasn't carrying a baby he said it gave him the green light to give me a good beating with the wooden cane if I ever dared to defend myself and I defended myself regularly.

I was awake most of the night with my daughter, but she eventually slept in my bed with me. I knew I had a lucky escape with Darren that evening, and I was still on high alert until the early hours of the morning, half expecting him to come back into the room once he'd heard I'd settled the baby, but thankfully he'd left me be and it wasn't until late the next evening when he'd returned with some food for me and a pouch of baby rice for Hope.

Darren didn't say anything when he dropped off my food, I assumed he was hungover which suited me as I was shattered from the night before, but I was right in thinking my baby girl was hungry. A few spoons of baby rice with her evening bottle and she was out like a light, I also got some much-needed sleep that night.

CHAPTER FORTEEN – Hope Everdeen, Aged 3

The sun was shining in through the skylight.

"Mummy the sun is saying hello, mummy! Please wake up."

Mummy said it was the Springtime and that some mornings if we were lucky the sunshine would come into our room to play. The sun made everything so happy. The way the light danced off the box in the corner of our room was special. Instead of the walls just being brown, they lit up with a rainbow of colours. I found myself tracing my hand across the wall.

Mum told I needed to be careful because sometimes bits of the wood get stuck in my fingers, and it could be really sore. The last time it happened, mum sucked on my finger until the bits of wall came out. She must have a belly full of wall by now because I didn't learn my lesson. Having a rainbow hand was worth the stinging fingers.

"Oh look, Mr Spider has come to play."

Mr Spider was my absolute best friend, after my mum of course. I think mum had made friends with my Mr Spider too, because she didn't hide on her bed when she saw him anymore. I don't know why she used to find him so scary, he didn't even bite, but mum said she had been scared of Mr Spider since she was little like me.

Mum told me she also had spiders in her house, before our house together. I have asked her about her Mr Spider, but mum didn't talk about him as much as I talked about my Mr. Spider.

"Mummy you will miss it."

"Okay, okay," she opened her eyes.

There she was, I liked it when my mummy first woke up in the mornings, she would smile at me and pull me into bed with her for our morning cuddles. My mummy always gives the best morning cuddles ever.

"Come over here monkey."

Mummy called me a monkey all of the times, used to be unsure what a monkey was, but she explained I didn't look like a hairy monkey, but I did act like one when I climbed all over the furniture. One day we were lucky to see a real one in the box. I watched them so closely and I guess I did a good monkey impression, even better since I practiced really hard. Mummy said she would take me to see a monkey in real life one day soon. I wondered what the 'real life' was, but it sounded exciting.

I loved the smell of mummy's hair in the mornings and the way it tickled my nose as I cuddled into her neck. She would whisper into my ear that she loved me and kissed me on the cheek. When it was time for us to both get up, mummy would help me to get dressed. The mornings were my favourite times.

It was breakfast time, so I grabbed my bowl out of the cupboard and set myself a place at the table. Mum always poured my cereal into my bowl for me, and she would reach into the fridge to get the milk, because I was still too small to reach it, I needed to be at least another head bigger.

"We need more milk; do you want to add it to the list?" mummy asked me.

"M... I... L.... K..." she spelt it out for me, so I could write it on our list.

"Very good Hope, you're writing is getting very neat."

"Thank you mummy."

I felt all happy inside when mummy would tell me that I've done something well, especially my writing because she said it was the most important thing out of all the important things she taught me. She told me she was like my teacher, and explained that when I got bigger, I might get the chance to go to a school where other people will teach me just like my mummy did.

My mummy talked about her old teachers and told me how much fun it was going to be. I wanted to go so badly because she made it sound magical, but mummy said we needed to get to the outside first, because that was where all the teachers lived. I wanted to have a teacher, but I also liked our little house; I didn't really want to go to the outside.

"Is the outside scary?" I asked.

Mummy smiled at me and pulled me tightly into her arms for a cuddle. We span around in a big circle together, dancing in the rainbow light. She told me the outside was a magical place and that she couldn't wait to show me all the special things the world had to offer. I didn't know what a world was, but I smiled at her because it seemed to make my mummy happy.

"After breakfast we can put the colour box on for a little while." She suggested.

The outside I was told was a little bit like our TV, only mummy said it was a lot bigger. I was a little bit confused when she told me that the people we saw in the TV were real people, because they seemed far too little to me, I looked at the back of the TV and I didn't see any little people, but my mummy assured me, she was right.
Maybe it was only mummy's who could see the little people. I thought about the outside a lot, and wondered if all of the outside was as tiny and small as the ones hiding in the back of our TV. Maybe I was a giant? I hoped not, I really didn't want to be a giant because the giant in my story book was big and very scary.

"I don't want to scare the Outside people mummy," I said, worried about the little people.

"The Outside will love you Hope Everdeen. Just as much as I do."

Mummy kissed me on the top of my head before lowering me back down to my seat. "Now eat up, before it goes soggy."

***

I was sat by the TV, which I still called the colour box, watching all of the different colours taking over the screen. Mummy told me I was watching a cartoon and she explained that the 'Outside' people would make lots of little drawings and put them all together, and magic would make them move. She said she was going to ask the nasty man for extra paper that weekend and she reminded me that it was almost my birthday.

I loved my birthday because that meant we were allowed to have cake again. We had cake when it was mummy's birthday, but mummy didn't like the cake and said it tasted stale, so I had extra. I wondered if mummy was going to like my cake this time. I really hoped so because cake was so yummy.

When the box got turned off, I laid myself down on the floor by our bed and I was trying to be very still, looking up at the skylight. Mummy then asked me what I was doing. I showed her. She came a lay on the floor beside me so she could see the same as me.

"What is that?" I asked.

"It looks like a leaf." Mum paused before looking back at me "A leaf from a tree."

"Like the tree on the colour box?" I asked.

"Exactly like that Jellybean."

My mummy paused for a minute and was looking up at the leaf for a little while longer before smiling at me and telling me it was time for my wash.

I was getting too big for the sink so instead of sitting on the countertop, mummy pulled out the chair for me to stand on.

"Ouch." I said as mummy touched my sore.

"Sorry princess."

I had a sore at the top of my arm from when I was climbing over the bed and slipped, because we heard the nasty man was coming down the wooden hill. The nasty man was not allowed to see me so when he knocked on our door, mum would ask me to hide in the wardrobe. That was my quiet space and I had all of my favourite things in there with me, like my soft blanket and the drawing of The Christmas Man that mummy made for me the first time I was too scared to go inside the wardrobe. Any time the nasty man came into our room, or if I felt myself getting scared, I could just look up at The Christmas Man and he would protect me, just like magic, and it worked too, just like my mummy said it would. The Christmas man had a big happy smile on his face and mummy told me he made a silly "Ho, Ho," noise.

The nasty man would knock the door usually but not last time, he just walked through the door without any warning and in a panic, I slipped off the bed and hit my arm of the side of the kitchen table. It was so sore, but I knew that I had to be silent otherwise he might have started shouting at me too. The nasty man shouted at my mummy all of the times.

"Is that bruise still there?" Mum asked.

It had started to turn yellow which I knew meant it was almost healed. "Almost gone." I smiled.

"I am so lucky to have you jellybean, I am sorry I cannot give you more." Mum looked sad again, I didn't like it when my mummy was sad.

CHAPTER FIFTEEN – Something had to change

With my daughter getting older and more inquisitive I found it harder to explain things to her in a way that she would understand, the last thing I would have ever wanted was for Hope to feel like she had missed out on anything. I knew she had nothing to compare her life to, but I did, and I knew what she was missing out on. Friends, a family, freedom were just a few things we were both missing out on, not that I had any friends or family, but I did unfortunately remember what freedom felt like and I missed it. I remembered how it felt to have the sun beating down on my skin, the way you could taste the fresh air on a crisp winters morning and the feeling of rain dripping down my face on a wet day. It was the simple things in life which most would take for granted, which I missed the most. I missed my freedom so much and being cooped up like a prisoner wasn't good enough anymore, especially for my little girl, who seemed far too innocent for the cruel world she'd been born into. I knew I had done all I could for her, but she deserved more, a hell of a lot more, we both did. We'd been forced to live with Darren for far too long and something needed to change.

I had hoped the man would've softened over time, but he didn't. He had to realise keeping us both captive was wrong and inhumane, but Darren had lost any grip with reality since the death of his son. He drank a lot, and I guessed it was his coping mechanism but drinking so much meant Darren had reverted back to his violent tendencies. My body was used to being beaten, well before Darren got his hands on me so as messed up as it may have sounded, I was okay with him taking his anger out on me, if it meant he left my daughter alone. Which worked for almost four years, and then one day he started demanding to see my daughter.

I had been able to shelter her from him for years and I wasn't about to give into him, just because of a few punches, because Darren also knew I would fight back just as hard. The more he drank, the worse his aggression would be, but it also meant the more unstable on his feet he'd be. So, half the time Darren would huff off back upstairs because starting on me wasn't as easy as he'd expected, making it boring for him.

The last time he tried to see my daughter, he threatened to take her off me, he regretted it when he was left with a lovely inch long scar on the top of his head where I hit him with one of our ceramic bowls. The broken bowl was never replaced but Hope and I managed fine sharing the same plastic bowl. It kept our room a little tidier too.

I was dreading it because I needed to have the horrible conversation about our shopping when I saw Darren next, the man liked to play games with me if I ever needed to ask for toiletries or if I needed anything for Hope and with her birthday approaching,

I had promised her a cake. I vowed to do everything in my power to never let her down, so when she asked if we were having a cake, I couldn't say no, could I? I just dreaded what the extra items on my list would cost me.

As I guessed Darren agreed to the extra items on my list, but he forced me to perform oral sex on him first. He done it just to control me and I don't believe he enjoyed it either, it was definitely more about the hold he had over me, than the man being turned on. Once he'd finished, he went and sat at my kitchen table and acted as if it were the most normal thing in the world. I hated the man with a passion and didn't hide it from him either.

"You make me sick." I told him.

"You're welcome Princess."

Just then I panicked as I realised Hope had left some stuff of hers on the kitchen table and Darren had the cheek to pick up one of my daughters drawings.

"Quite the little artist we have here." he smirked.
"We?" I said, "she is my child."

"You cannot hide her from me forever you know, soon enough she won't fit in there." He looked over at the wardrobe and a cold shiver ran down my spine.

"I can, and I will." I snapped.

"I will meet her one day." He sniggered, looking down at the drawing of a tree. "I'm basically like her dad."

"You'll never meet her, and she is my daughter, she is nothing to do with you Darren." I shouted, angry at his cheek.

"Do you pay for her?" he asked but I didn't respond. "What if I buy her a present, then she will have to see me to thank me, wouldn't she?"

The man was having a laugh; Darren wouldn't think of anyone but himself and he sure as hell wasn't planning on buying my child a present. At least I didn't want him to.

"If you come here and sit on this." He said pointing to his crouch. "I will buy her a cutesy little teddy bear." Darren was an idiot and raised his voice purposely to make sure Hope could hear him, but little did he know my daughter wore a pair of earmuffs to drown out any unwelcome noises.

Darren was gross, a perverted old man, but he tried to convince himself otherwise. He convinced himself that I was secretly attracted to him and they told me he knew I wanted to be with him romantically. He was deluded to think so, but I believe it was all part of his messed-up mind game, just like everything else.

When he first started raping me, I was to pretend I was enjoying myself to help speed up the whole ordeal, if Darren thought I was lying to him, and realised how much he made my skin crawl he had gone ape shit, but the truth was he made my insides repel at the thought of him. Although if I'd not done a good enough job at convincing him I was enjoying myself, it would have resulted in a server beating as well. It was a lot easier to play along with his games half of the time, easier on my body, but not so easy on my mind.

"You are lucky I have other things to do, otherwise I would have you riding me like the good little whore you are."

I didn't say anything, it was easier that way, at first I would argue back but with Hope in the room, and only metres away from us both, I didn't chance it. Instead, I kept my mouth shut.

Within minutes Darren was up on his feet and informing me he was turning the electric off on us in an hour, so I best fed my child while I had the chance. The electric being switched off was originally given to me as a punishment for answering him back a few years previously, but he enjoyed the control it had over me, especially in the winter months.

Thankfully, we had a few candles and Hope, and I would enjoy making up stories around the candle and pretend we were out camping in the woods. It didn't matter what Darren tried; he could never beat me, mentally I was stronger than him, but I guess I had to be. I was thankful that I made of strong stuff and that was one of Darren's biggest issues with me. I think the man thought he could break me, but I knew he'd break well before me, because I had everything to live for and he had nothing. Nothing but two prisoners locked up in his basement and an awfully long prison sentence if he were ever to be caught.

CHAPTER SIXTEEN – Birthday girl

Mummy told me it was my birthday the next day and I was going to be a big four-year-old. We wrote out our shopping list for the nasty man and mum added some ingredients for a cake. Normally he wouldn't allow such things on our list, but he knew it was my birthday because he was there the day I was born. Our tiny home belonged to him, and he was in charge of everything we did.

"If we make your cake tonight, it means we can have cakes for breakfast, otherwise he might sleep in, which means we'll have no power in the morning again." Mummy explained.

"Cake for breakfast?" My eyes lit up at the thought of such a special treat.

I was so lucky to have my mummy, she was always so thoughtful. Maybe that was why she was my mummy.

"Can I be a mummy one day?" I asked.

She looked at me and laughed. "Not until you are at least thirty."

I tried to count on my hands, but I lost count. Mummy told me it was three lots of big hands. That sounded incredibly old to me.

"Mummy, you are not three hands old." I said confused.

"No Baby, I am not. But do as I say, not as I do." She smiled. "That was something your grandmother used to say to me when I was little."

"Your mummy?" I asked.

"Yes."

I was little confused by that comment. If my mummy, had her own mummy. *Why was she not living in her mummy's house?*

"Where is your mummy?" I asked.

"My Mummy lives in a place called Manchester. When we get out of here we might visit Manchester so you can see where Mummy used to live."

"Really?" I asked excitedly, I couldn't contain myself, and excited about seeing my mummy's, mummy, "is she like you?" I guessed that all of the mummy's were like mine.

"I am not sure; I haven't seen her in a while."

"Can we see your mummy, can we?" I asked.

"We will see Jellybean, while we are here, we won't be seeing anyone."

I felt bad because my mummy had tears in her eyes.

"I am sorry for making you sad." I reached out my arms and placed them around my mummy's shoulders.

She always had a big cuddle for me when I was sad, it was my time to give one back. Mummy squeezed me back.

"You didn't make me sad princess, you never could."

***

I was stood on the chair which made me almost as tall as my mummy. I smiled, a proud grin as I passed her the ingredients we needed to make my birthday cake. Once she cracked the eggs, I waiting for her to give me the shells, like she always did but for some reason she placed all of the shells into some toilet paper and then put it up high, on the top shelve where we had all of our tins of food.

I looked at her, wondering why she didn't just ask me to put them in the binbag as usual. Shells were rubbish and we couldn't eat them.

"It might come in handy." She said as if she knew exactly what I was thinking.

I nodded my head. My mummy somehow always knew what I was thinking. She was magic and that was why I loved her. Well one of lots and lots of reasons. Once all the ingredients were in the bowl, mummy slid the bowl over to me. It was my job to stir it all together. I was stirring as hard as I could, but the gloopy mess was going everywhere, all over mummy and me.

"Slow down a little." Mum advised me, placing her hand around mine to show me how to do it slowly.

Mummy started laughing because she ended up getting cake mix in her hair because I was still stirring to fast, I was excited to be making cake. Mummy then scooped a big dollop of the mix on her fingertip and smudged it on the end of my nose. We both started laughing and making even more mess. By the time we'd calmed down and placed the cake mix into the tray, mummy said we had wasted half of the mixture all down ourselves.

"It may be smaller than we expected, but it is going to taste heavenly." She smiled at me before placing the cake tin into our extremely hot oven.

"Is the nasty man having any of our cake?" I asked.

Mummy told me that the nasty man had been far too badly behaved to be allowed any of our cake, because only good people were allowed birthday cake, and the nasty man didn't know how to be well behaved, that was why he was called 'the nasty man.' He was also nasty to my mummy, so I didn't like him.

***

The next morning, I woke up and I was even bigger, now that I was four years old. I was super excited because we had a lovely vanilla flavoured cake for breakfast, just like my mummy had promised. I also got a new colouring book and some colourful crayons, and I even impress myself by knowing all the colours without any help which proved I was a big girl.

I was sat at the table and showing mummy just how carefully I could colour in, without going over the lines. I used to be a little rubbish at keeping the colour behind the lines, but I had already coloured in two other pictures that morning and it was agreed that when I finished the lasted one I was working on, we could put them up on the wall. Mummy had a butterfly to colour in; I had an apple with a naughty caterpillar who took a big bite of the apple without asking permission.

"Are all caterpillars naughty?" I asked.

"Not all of them, and why is your caterpillar naughty?"

"Because he took a bite of the apple." I explained.

"Ah, I see. He might have just been hungry." Mummy told me.

"But he didn't ask first."

I heard her giggle, but I was right by a black line, and didn't want to lose my concentration. When I was happy with my work, I looked back up at her. Mummy was smiling away to herself. I liked it when she was smiling because it meant she was happy.

"I am nearly finished." She said signing her name at the bottom of the finished masterpiece. *Siobhan Everdeen, Aged 17.*

When I signed my own picture, I almost forgot it was my birthday and I wrote down that I was three, then mummy reminded me that I need to write number four down from then on.

"Shall we put them up on the wall?"

I looked around our room, deciding where the best place was to put up our pretty pictures. We didn't have much choice apart from over the bed. The other side of the room had the wardrobe and the kitchen cupboards, and the pictures were too big to go beside the sink.

"I think…" I said taking another look before finalising my decision. "I think Mr Caterpillar can go there." I pointed to just above our headboard. "Butterfly and cat can go there." I pointed to the area above the bed.

Bang! Bang! Bang!

The loud noise startled me, and I started to cry. Mummy quickly jumped off the bed to tried and console me, but I was scared.

"It is only the man, be a big girl and go wait in the wardrobe." She kissed me on the head.

"But I…" The tears were instant and started to drip down my cheeks.

"Please Hope, you know the rules."

I listened to her and climbed into the wardrobe like I'd been asked but I wasn't happy. I made sure the blanket was in the way of the door ever so slightly, so I had enough of a gap to see through the doors. I was not scared of the dark, but I didn't like it much either.
I watched as my mum walked towards the door and stood waiting for the nasty man to let himself in. I couldn't see either of them, but I could hear him talking to her. He was talking about my birthday and a part of me started to get excited and wondered if he had a gift for me. Then I heard my mummy telling him to go away. He shouted at her and then I saw my mum falling on the bed. She screamed for him to leave.

"I want to see her, don't be such a spoilsport."

"You promised me you'll leave her alone, you promised."

Mum got off the bed and I saw the back of the nasty man's head. It looked like he grabbed her by the hair and said something in her ear, but I couldn't hear what was being said. I was very scared for my mummy. I didn't like it when the nasty man was ever in our room. He always made my mummy cry.

He made me jump when he slammed his hand down on our table really hard and walked back towards the door. I could just see his arm as he pointed to my mum.

"You're going to wish you hadn't been so rude to me." He shouted.

Our room went silent again and a few minutes passed before my mummy told me I was allowed back out. I ran straight over to her, to give her a big cuddle. Mummy always cuddled me when I was sad, so I wanted to help her again. It was like being a big four-year-old gave me extra cuddling powers.

"It is okay, I will look after you mummy." I said, just then, the lights got turned off.

"Looks like we have no electric again today, luckily we still have cake. Do you want to get the candles ready for when it gets darker later?" Mum asked.

"Sure."

I jumped down off the bed and collected the candles from underneath the sink. Mum didn't like it when the nasty man turned off the electric, but I loved watching the flame of the candles dance, so I was eagerly waiting for it to get darker so mum would light them up. She told me that when we had our own place, we could have our own fire and she said she would light it up every night before bedtime. I couldn't wait until we had our own place. It always sounded so nice and talking about it made my mummy smile, so it had to be a good thing.

CHAPTER SEVENTEEN – Planning for the future

Darren had informed me he was going away for the weekend, but he forgot to mention that we'd have no power for that weekend either. I'd managed to keep the milk fresh enough for Hope's breakfast by placing the carton in chilly water, but we had no way of heating up food, so for dinner that night we had outdated cold baked beans, direct from the can and a slice of stale bread each. It didn't help that we were approaching the winter, so not only did it get dark by the early evening, but it was freezing cold. With no electric, I had no way of heating the place up, usually I would have turned the oven on for half an hour to take the chill out of the air, but I couldn't do anything, apart from layer us both up. We were even fresh out of candles and Darren's latest mood meant any extra items on our shopping list, were rejected, which included my sanitary towels and tea light candles.

    I felt terrible and a failure as a mother because Hope had started getting the sniffles, and I knew there wasn't anything I could do to help her, It was hard to not see yourself as a shit mother, when I couldn't even keep my kid warm, I knew it wasn't my fault, but it didn't stop me from feeling like a useless waste of space. My mind had started to wonder off into its own world trying to think of ways of getting us out of there, but with a door to a locked-up house between us, it wasn't going to be easy.

I managed to make a weapon, but I wasn't convinced my makeshift knife would cut it, it was made from gluing a load of eggshells together and attaching it to our wooden spoon. *How was that going to work?* I didn't think it would do enough damage to hurt anything, let alone pierce the skin. I'd tried it out on my own arm, and it left a little mark, but the force I would have needed to seriously hurt Darren, was beyond me.

Darren was far from stupid and didn't ever let me own a knife, or anything sharp that I could have used against him, because the last time he'd trusted me, was with the ceramic bowl and I had left him bloodied. After that he removed most of the things out of my room to avoid it happening again. Even our plates and the single bowl we owned were made of plastic, and I tried to break them in the past too, but they just bent and turned a lighter coloured plastic. Our plastic cutlery and that never did look the same again, but it still worked. Escaping was never going to be easy, but that didn't stop me from trying.

One of the days, I had tried acting like I was really sick, telling Darren I needed to go to the hospital, but the man would have rather seen me dead, than let anyone know about me. I had the flu at the time, but I played on it to the point, even poor Hope was convinced I was really ill. Trying to explain to a toddler, that I was okay, was harder than trying to convince Darren that I wasn't. From that moment I decided that I couldn't involve my daughter in my escape plan, and it was something I needed to do on my own, for the sake of us both.

***

Monday finally came around and by that point Hope and I were more than grateful to have some heating back in our room, it snowed over that weekend, and we only knew that because the whole of Sunday we had spent it in complete darkness as the snowfall covered the tiny skylight above us. At times that little skylight was our only source of light and my only indication to what day of the week it was, otherwise, I would've been completely clueless. The winter at least seemed milder than the previous year where we had a cold spell that brought snow to us in the middle of May and the summer months seemed to fly by so quickly.

Time for me usually dragged ninety percent of the time, days could really go on when you were stuck indoors with only a child to keep you from losing your mind. Hope helped me in ways I couldn't comprehend, I think her just being there with me, cracking jokes and being cute as hell, was my medicine. I would have given up if it weren't for my daughter. I loved being her mother, more than I had ever loved anything in my life and I just wanted better for her, because she deserved better.

I was sat at the table colouring in with my little girl when I heard the knock on the door. Darren shouted into me to warn me that he was about to enter, which usually gave me enough time to coax Hope into the wardrobe.

"I don't want to mummy." She complained.

"You know the rules Jellybean, just for a little while."

"But…"

Tears started to form behind her eyes, as I picked her up into my arms, the door knocked again. "One minute." I shouted.

"No mummy, no… Please." She begged but she knew the rules and I hadn't the time to argue with a four-year-old.

Before Hope turned four years old, she would have happily headed into the wardrobe with zero issues, if anything, she found hiding in her 'special place' a treat, but just before her birthday, she'd started acting like I was dishing out a punishment. I knew the day would come that she'd become too big for the cramped space, but I didn't expect that day to happen so soon.

"Hope Everdeen, stop this now. Just hide for me, I promise it won't be for long."

The door behind me opened and I panic as Hope was still in my arms. Darren entered the room, and I heard his voice; so, I turned my body away from him, to shield my daughter. I had my back to the man, but I could feel him inching closer to us.

"There she is." His voice was slimy, and sent a cold shiver down my spine. "Let me take a proper look at her."

"Stay away from her." I warned, hearing his footsteps getting even closer to us.

"Hope please just wait in here for me." I placed my daughter in the wardrobe, on top of her blanket and closed the door, standing in front of it so she couldn't just open it and jump out.

"You are one mean mother," Darren sniggered at me. "She clearly wants to meet me."

It didn't help that Hope was crying her little heart out and I tried to calm her with my words, but Darren carried on walking closer to me. I stepped away from the wardrobe. Hoping he'd follow my lead, thankfully Hope stayed in her hiding place.

"You have no business with her, you promised you would leave her alone." I reminded him, but Darren had that glazed look in his eyes, something was about to happen. I could feel it with every ounce of my being, but I was actually ready for it for once. Adrenaline was taking over my body and I was about to do everything in my power, to keep his dirty hands and sleazy eyes away from my little girl.

Darren ignored my warnings and made his way over my crying child, but I stood in the way of the doors again, just in time.

"Move out of the way." He shouted, trying to push me out of the way, but I stood my ground and got a fist to the stomach as a reward. He might have winded me, but I stood back up quickly and warned him again that it was in his best interests to leave my daughter alone. I felt invincible in that moment, stood there pumping out my chest, like that was going to help me in some way.

"Or what? What are you going to do?" He laughed in my face and pulled me by the arm, dragging me away from the wardrobe doors.
"Make me." He sniggered.

My fist collided with Darren's chest at first, I repeatedly hit him with both of my hands, pushing him away from the wardrobe but he grabbed my arm and twisted it around my back. He pulled me into his arms and all I could smell was the stale whiskey on his breath. It turned my stomach, the smell lingered in the air as he whispered into my ear, warning me that I'd just crossed the line. Before I knew it I was on the floor, Darren laying ten tons of living shit out of me. I covered my face as usual as Darren continued to kick me in the stomach and then he stamped on my leg. I screamed out in pain, but he carried on kicking me on the floor.
"Leave my mummy alone!" I heard Hope shouting, and I knew I needed to get my beaten arse up off the floor before his attention turned solely onto her.

Darren turned around just as Hope jumped out of the wardrobe, she was stood there with her hands on her hips and if the moment weren't so serious, I would have seen the cuteness in her defending her mummy. I managed to get myself onto my knees and in the corner of my eye, I notice my makeshift knife stuffed under the mattress. I knew I was too far away to grab it so, I pulled myself up to my feet and watched on helplessly as Darren picked up my baby girl. He then turned towards the door and for a second, I thought he was about to take my baby girl from me.

Hope was screaming my name and all of a sudden I saw red. *No one was taking my daughter away from me. Ever!* I reached for the eggshell knife and ran at him, repeatedly attempting to stab him, anywhere I could. Plunging my makeshift knife so hard, I could feel bits of the eggshell braking off in my hands.

He released his grip on Hope and she fell to the floor. Darren then turned his attention onto me, but I need to make sure my daughter was okay. She was crying and I could see blood on her, and for a split second I thought it was her blood, that maybe I had accidently marked her in my outraged attack and it filled me with guilt.

It wasn't my daughters blood thankfully, and I saw that as soon as Darren turned around to face me, he was holding onto his neck, blood seeping through his hand. He looked at me, his face was as white as a ghost and I noticed a fear in his eyes, a look I hadn't seen before. I pulled Hope away from Darren, and she hid herself down in-between the bed and wardrobe.

Darren turned and lunged himself at me, the rage was back in his eyes as he came at me again. I moved myself to create a human shield between Hope and that monstrous man. Who seemed a lot less scary with blood seeping from his neck. I realised I hadn't caused enough damage to immobilise him, but I was secretly proud of myself for even being able to hurt him. This was our one and only chance to make a run for it, because I knew Darren wasn't about to let me get away with hurting him, I was going to pay with my own blood and knowing that had me I refusing to back down. He would have to kill me before he got the chance to spend time with my baby and I told him just as much. Which made him attempt to attack me again.

I panicked and pulled out the chair from the table and placed it in front of the both of us, using it to protect myself as Darren tried to grab me again, but to no avail. Which only resulted in me pissing him off even more. I felt empowered, finally strong enough to take one the drunken excuse for a man.

Hope was screaming behind me as I swung the chair towards Darren, missing him completely which frustrated me to tears. I screamed out, hoping someone, anyone would hear us, but I also knew, no one would. I had tried that tactic in the past and it never worked.

Darren stumbled towards me, he almost fell to the ground but composed himself and advanced straight at me. He managed to grab hold of my hair and pulled me in close. His breath was brushing against my cheek, as I tried to headbutt him, but I completely missed.

"You're dead." He warned.

"Not if I can help it."

The makeshift knife was on the floor by the door, and I tried to reach for it, but Darren pulled my hair even tighter. He was spitting threats in my ear, telling me my daughter was about to be an orphan. I reached out again but Darren saw what I was trying to retrieve and reached down to grab it before I had chance to. He started mocking me on my poor attempts of weaponry, but that weapon had already hurt him, and I realised it was a pretty nasty gash on his neck which looked pretty deep.

The hair pulling had never bothered me, I had thick hair anyway, so it didn't hurt. I tried to kick out at him, but I felt something on the back of my leg as Hope slid herself underneath me and ran to hide under the table. Darren grabbed me with the broken egg and spoon in his hand, but I was able to wiggle free and only just manage avoiding him lunging it at me.

A table stood between us as Darren lunged at me again, dropping what was left of my broken knife on the floor. I ran to grab it before he did. My knees skimmed the floor, but I managed to get hold of it and got myself back behind the table before he could grab me.

"You stupid cow." He hissed at me.

Hope was hidden underneath the table, I saw her shaking, terrified and I needed to end the situation, but the only way I knew how, was to put Darren down, once and for all. I ran towards him, swinging at him, swinging in every direction. I felt my hand collide with his body and within seconds Darren was laying on the floor. I was a little proud of myself, thinking I had managed to get him on the ground, but little did I know that my amazing daughter had only just gone and tied his shoelaces together unnoticed, so when Darren tried to come at me, he tripped over his own feet, landing in a heap on the floor and hitting his head in the process.

I looked at Hope and signalled for her to turn around as I didn't want her to see me laying ten tons of shit into the nasty son of a bitch who'd held me captive. Darren felt five whole years of pent-up aggression as I took pleasure in stamping on his face repeatedly, just like he tried to do to me countless of times in the past. By the third foot to the face, he was completely immobile. Laying there unresponsive, the impact from my foot against his smug face, clearly opening the wound in his neck further and I watched on for a second, watching him as he bled out in front of me. For a second, I wondered if Darren had felt the same feeling as me, the day he watched his own son bleed out. It looked like history was about to repeat itself.

"A little DeJa'Vu?" I sniggered before watching him struggle for breath. *Was I about to kill him?*

I felt no remorse, which I maybe should have felt at least something, but in that moment, the man deserved everything he got, and then some. I think I was in some state of shock because it took for Hope to come running up to my legs and wanting picked up into my arms before I realised the implications of what had just happened.

I was convinced I had just killed my abductor, I felt strong and empowered but that panicked me a little because I wasn't a killer, well not until that day, I wasn't. How could I look at my daughter in the eyes after that? I was protecting her, but in doing that I had become something I never expected to be, a murderer. It was in self-defence, but it didn't make a difference to me.

I scooped up my daughter into my arms and limped over towards the door, it was our chance to finally escape, and I was running with it.

"Shit!" I swore in frustration.

The door was locked obviously, so I placed Hope back down to her feet and walked back over to Darren body. I knew the keys were in his jeans pocket, but I was scared as I got closer to his body.

"Careful mummy."

I was just about to grab the set of keys when Darren regained consciousness and grabbed hold of my arm. He looked me deep in the eyes, not saying a word and for a split second I was in a trance, then he tried to move and moaned out in pain. I had to finish the job, so I reached for the broken egg stick and stabbed him in the chest as hard as I could.

The wooden spoon wasn't up to the task, breaking in my hand and splitting my own finger open in the process but Darren's body went limp nevertheless, the impact was enough to knock him out and I was able to get to Hope and open the door to our room without him moving.

We made our way upstairs to the other part of the house and I placed Hope back on her own two feet, then both of us ran straight to the locked front door. I fumbled with the keys, although none of the keys wanted to fit into the extra-large padlock. Darren had eight keys on his set, one could be ruled out because it was for his car, the rest were for different doors throughout the house, but not one of them was the right key for the front door. For a second I felt trapped.

"The back door." I said, but Hope had no idea what I meant so I picked her up into my arms again.

I walked us through the kitchen, but I was sure I could hear noises coming from my dungeon below us but thankfully the first key I tried had fit the back door and it swung open with the wind, banging against the wall behind it.

Hope gasped as the chilly air hit us, but it was the best feeling in the world to me. I didn't care that I had no shoes on or that there was still small spots of ice and snow on the ground, all I cared about was getting us both as far away from that house as possible. I contemplated seeing if the car would start up, but I didn't know the first thing about driving. I'd only ever been a passenger in a taxi, so the car seemed like the more dangerous option.

CHAPTER EIGHTEEN – With Hope comes Freedom

We ran so fast towards the trees, the same trees I had fantasied about for so long. I was running that fast that my legs no longer felt attached to my body which I was slightly glad of because Darren had really hurt my leg when he'd stamped on it, although Hope was getting heavier by the second and I needed to stop, but I was also too scared to. The freezing cold ground had numbed my feet to the point of hurting but I still wasn't about stop. I continued running, far too scared to even look behind us. I was paranoid that Darren would be in hot pursuit and the last thing I needed was panic to cloud my judgement. Hope was still sobbing but I tried to convince her that we were free, it didn't dawn on me at first but that was Hope's first time being outdoors and it was already scary for her. I told her that she had me there as always and she knew I would do everything in my power to protect her. She was shaking, a mix of coldness and fear which meant she refused to let me put her down, I pulled her in tightly and reassured that everything was going to be okay. She buried her head into the nook of my neck and sobbed quietly. I hated that my baby girl was so upset, but it was soon going to be over.

Silent Hope | Sarah Louise Rosmond

The small forest area came to an end, and we found ourselves facing a big open field. I had no idea where I was going, what direction was best to take so I just kept running until I couldn't run any further.

My arms were sore from carrying Hope in my arms for so long, and I needed to place her down on the ground while I caught my breath. My poor baby girl still looked petrified, but she was no longer crying.

"You're okay." I reassured her, but she stayed quiet.

Once I regained my breath, I picked her up again and we made our way across the large open field. I couldn't run anymore, I didn't have it in me, although I walked as quickly as physically possible until we finally stumbled upon a country road. The road was deserted but I was still fearful of Darren catching up to us. I didn't believe he'd come after us on foot, but he owned a car, an old green Rover sat on the man's driveway, but whether or not it was a running vehicle, I couldn't have told you. I'd never heard the thing get started up so with any luck, it was a nonrunner. In a panic to leave the hell house, I lobbed the set of keys that I took from Darren, into the bushes outside his garden, making it more difficult for him to find them. Even so, the fear was enough to make me want to stay out of sight.

Hope and I walked behind the hedges to conceal ourselves from any passing cars.

"My feet hurt Mummy." Hope was on the verge of crying again, but we were so close to being free, I couldn't let us stop.

"I know darling, mine too but we need to keep moving."

"Where are we?" she asked, and I explained we were in the outside as she called it, and I tried to convince her that we were going to be fine, and I was there to keep her safe.

I didn't feel safe, anything but, although I wanted Hope to enjoy the thought of us being outside, after all I had promised her that we would go on adventures as soon as we were able to get outside, so I didn't want her any more scared of it, than she already was. It wasn't the way I'd hoped she'd experience freedom, but we were on the verge of being free, I could taste it.

"Do you remember me talking about our adventures?" I asked and her little eyes lit up. "Well, this is like an adventure and nothing to be sad about, mummy is here."

Four-year-olds ask a lot of questions, and my daughter was no exception, as much as I was trying my hardest to keep calm, I didn't have all the answers, and that frustrated Hope even more. Mummy always knew what to say, but in that moment I had no idea what I was supposed to feel, never mind knowing what the right thing was to say. I was too preoccupied with keeping a look out, that I was no fun for my daughter, who sulked at me.

I knew it would never be easy staying with Darren from day one, but the man had become more and more volatile, and after my attack on him, he'd be out for blood. Entertaining my child was the least of my priorities.

We had been walking for what seemed like hours when a car appeared in the distance, I was in two minds whether or not to hide, but I could see it was a silver car, and not a green Rover.

Hope had calmed down during that time and was walking hand in hand with me, both of us quiet and deep in thought. Hope was knackered and you could see it in her face, we needed to rest.

Seeing the car slowly approaching us gave me the urge to stand on the side of the road, and wave my arms frantically like they did in the American movies I'd watched growing up. Hope started mimicking me, and I couldn't help but smile at my brave little sidekick.

I wasn't even sure hitchhiking was a good idea and whether it would even work in England but thankfully, the car slowed down and pulled up on the other side of the road. I could see it was a female driver and it looked like she was on her own. She put down her window and shouted.

"Can I help you?"

"Please we need a ride." I shouted.

"Excuse me." She said.

I should have known hitchhiking wouldn't work but I needed her help.

"Please help us," I sounded like I was begging, "my name is Siobhan Everdeen, and I was abducted five years ago. We've just escaped." I explained.

"Oh my." She gasped in horror, the woman instantly felt awkward, and it was obvious that she didn't know where to look.

Hope and I made our way across the road. The woman asked me a few questions before getting out of the car, including asking me who the little girl was. The look on the woman's face when I explained Hope was my child, said all that it needed to know. I was seventeen and I knew I looked young for my age, but I felt like the woman was looking down on me, then she asked Hope if I was telling the truth, which pissed me off, she didn't believe me. *Why would I have lied to her?* After questioning me further, she looked down at Hope and reluctantly agreed to help us.

She opened the car door for us, and both climbed into the back seat of the car. I helped Hope to put on her seatbelt, which she thought was amazing. My daughter had never even seen a car, never mind travelled in one and she was quiet, but smiling and clearly observing everything around us.

The kind woman asked me where I was from, I told her, she then explained Manchester was the other side of the county and the best she could do for us, was drop me off at the nearest police station. The thought of taking to the police was daunting to say the least, and I was scared I would be in trouble for murdering Darren.

I was asked a lot of questions on that journey, and I was sure I would be having to answer the exact same questions when I got to the police station, so the last thing I wanted to do, was to go through it all with her as well. I wasn't being rude, but I felt like she was just being nosey for the sake of it. She came across like a local gossip and I didn't feel comfortable with sharing any details with her. I believed she was the type to be telling everyone about her exciting passengers for the day and I wasn't going to be headlining her gossip party.

I was grateful for the ride, grateful that my daughter and I could finally rest our feet for a few minutes, but I also couldn't wait to be as far away as possible from it all. I was shattered, and so was Hope. I wondered whether the police would protect us. I guessed they would have to help us find somewhere to sleep otherwise we would have to sleep rough. The weather was far too harsh to sleep on the streets and I couldn't do that to my baby girl. The police station seemed like my only option.

"I am sorry, you both must be knackered, listening to me going on." The woman said, clearly seeing I was deep in thought. I didn't respond, I just looked out of the window, thankful to finally be free.

CHAPTER NINETEEN – Finally Free

The woman dropped us both off just outside the police station and I was so apprehensive about entering the building. *What would happen to Hope if I got arrested for attacking Darren?* We had no other option and regardless of what was going to happen to me, I knew the police would protect my daughter, so I tried to put all my doubts to the back of my mind and picked up Hope and we made our way inside.

The reception was busy, so I waited my turn. I might have been paranoid, but it felt like everyone was staring at us. Hope was obliviously looking around her, taking in her surroundings. Smiling away to herself but still noticeably quiet. I was grateful that she was no longer upset.

"Can I help you?" The officer behind the reception desk asked.

I didn't want the whole building to hear me, so I made my way over to the desk and lent forward to explain who I was and why we were there.

"Let me take some details off you." The officer said grabbing a notepad, "take a seat over there and we will be with you soon." He pointed behind us to a row of blue plastic seats.

Hope and I took a seat over at the other end of the waiting room. I still felt eyes on us coming from every direction. It was clear that I was being judged by everyone in that room and it was starting to get under my skin. I was ready to say something but instead I talked Hope into sticking her tongue out with me. It was childish but it made both me and Hope happy, for a few minutes at least.

"Is this our new home?" Hope asked me.

"No, Jellybean. I am hoping these lovely people are going to help us find a new home," she smiled at me, "and it won't just be a room this time, it will be a whole house, just like I've promised you."

"What about Mr Spider? We left him in our room." Hope said looking back down at her feet dangling off the chair.

"We can get a new Mr Spider." I explained and she was more than happy with that compromise.

I was so grateful that my daughter was dealing with the whole situation in such a grown-up way, whereas I just wanted to break down and cry. I stopped myself from welling up because I knew if I let the flood gates open, I would have cried for weeks on end. Mainly down to the feeling of relief.

"Miss Everdeen?" I female officer called my name. "This is Sandra, she works with children's services. With your permission she will take your little girl into a different room to play while we speak with you in private." She said.

I placed my arms around Hope, scared stiff to let her out of my sight for even a split second. "Is that really necessary?" I asked.

"Unfortunately, it is the best thing for your daughter, we just need to determine that you are both okay. I promise you it won't take long." She paused and looked at me, but I just shook my head. "Miss Everdeen, I can assure you she will be safe, and you will be in the very next room."

"She is safer with me." I snapped.

I didn't mean to be awkward, but I had no idea who the two women were, they could be anyone for all I knew. It was my job to protected my daughter, and for four years and done a fairly decent job, all things considering.

I was the only person Hope had ever known, and they were expecting me to let her out of my sight. Over my dead body. I wasn't prepared to let a complete stranger take my little girl away from me, and I told the police officer, just as much. I told them that Hope hadn't met another human until that day, which was true, apart from me and that monster who'd kept us captive, she known no one. The police officer looked a little bewildered. I had shielded Hope from everything, I had taught her all she knew, and I didn't feel comfortable having her out of my sight for even a split second.

Everyone was staring at me with their judging eyes, *maybe going to the police station wasn't the best idea.* All I wanted to do was pick up my daughter and walk back out of the station, but as I got up to my feet I was stopped from leaving, and told I needed to be interviewed before I could leave.

"Am I under arrest?" I asked sarcastically.

"No, but we need to make sure you are both safe." The woman from Children's Services said.

A male police officer came over to us and informed me that I needed to let them talk with me before I was allowed to leave. I was told I didn't have much choice in the matter as they needed to interview me, to make sure I wasn't a danger to myself, or anyone else. I was annoyed, they clearly thought I had lost the plot and as usual I was trapped yet again!

"Hope will be in the next room, can you come with me to interview room four please." The female officer placed her hand around my elbow, and coaxed me away from my daughter.

"She needs me, you don't understand." I shouted but I was ignored.

Hope jumped down from her chair and asked about the other police officers uniform. She was ignored at first, but the social worker acknowledged her eventually and answered Hope's question.

"Ms Everdeen, I assure you. We all have your best interests at heart, and all we are going to do is talk. That's it." The well-dressed woman gave me a sympathetic look, as if that were going to convince me.

"Why can't you talk to us together then." I stated, firmly standing my ground literally as the female officer was still trying to lead me away, but I broke free and ran straight back to my daughters side.

"Just leave her a second," I heard the male police officer talking to his colleague.

The two police officers and the social worker spoke briefly between themselves for a few minutes, I hated that they were talking about us and wanted to know what they were saying but instead, I looked down at Hope and reassured her that everything would be okay. I told my daughter that I wasn't going anywhere without her. She smiled at me, and grabbed hold of my hand, squeezing it tightly.

"Love you mummy." Her big eyes melting me as usual.

"I love you too Jellybean."

"Ms Everdeen, I have spoken to my boss, and she assures me that it is in your best interest to speak with me, without your daughter present. Unfortunately, if you do not let us speak to you in private, away from your daughter, it will look bad on you as a parent." She explained, "do you understand what I am saying?"

I let out a big sigh, I wanted them to know I wasn't impressed but without aggravating them further. I felt defeated, annoyed even because they had me over a barrel, and I knew it. Hearing stories about social services over the years, gave me a natural fear over them. They were branded as the organisation who took your kids off you, and at times I'd heard they did so using the most ridiculous of reasons. Not the type of people I wanted to put my trust in, that was something I was certain about.

"So, who are you?" I asked the women's names again.

Sandra introduced herself and explained she was from Children's Services and was there to make sure both Hope and I felt safe and protected.

"Children's Services?" I rolled my eyes at the woman; did she really think I was going to trust a social worker? Like I said, I had heard enough horror stories about those people growing up, I had zero faith in them.

"We are only here to help and support you Siobhan." Sandra explained but I still didn't trust either of them.

I looked around me to take myself away from the glaring stare of Sandra only to see everyone else looking and talking between themselves. I was definitely the hot topic of the day. I was in-flight mode and all that was going through my mind, was to keep running, but looking down at Hope, her big brown eyes burning themselves into my soul and I realised I needed to do what is best for her, regardless of how I felt myself.

Reluctantly I agreed to talking in private but asked if I could have a few minutes with my daughter on her own before they took her away.

"I am sorry but until we interview you Miss Everdeen, we can't leave you both alone." The police officer warned, "It is just protocol, nothing to be worried about."

"Are you having a laugh!" I snapped.

"You will both see each other very soon." Sandra turned to me, before lowing herself to my daughter's eye level. "Do you like drawing Hope?" She asked, and I watched as my daughter's eyes lit up in an instant.

"It's our favourite thing to do." I said, feeling a little ganged up on.

"Can I colour in mummy?" Hope asked excitedly and how in the hell could I have said no to her? Sandra was a clever woman, and she knew exactly what she was doing.

"Of course, you can Jellybean, mummy will just be talking to this police lady in the other room, while you colour in."

She hugged me, the biggest hug ever and I kissed her on the forehead, "Thank you mummy."

I felt like I was on the verge of losing her, and it seemed foolish but as soon as I had agreed to talking in private, I knew I had messed everything up. Once I was on my own, my emotions started boiling over and I finally broke down into floods of tears.

I was overthinking, worried that it was going to be the last time I saw my daughter, especially when the police found out that I murdered Darren in cold blood. I wasn't a murderer, but the police didn't know that.

I wondered if leaving Darren's was a good idea because at least with him I knew what to expect, but as usual, I even messed that up.

It wasn't until I was sat in the interview room on my own when I realised what all of those people must've been thinking. I looked a complete mess, neither Hope or I had any shoes on because we didn't own shoes, Darren didn't see the point, because he never planned on allowing either of us out and both of us had blood over our clothes from my fight with Darren. My feet were filthy and bloodied from all of the running through the woods and my bottoms were ripping at the seams, I had definitely seen better days. Hope's dress at least looked like it fitted her, whereas my own clothes were always a few sizes too big. I must've looked like I'd just crawled out of a grave. It was no wonder everyone had been staring at me. I would've stared at myself too had the shoe been on the other foot.

I was sat on my own, in a pool of self-doubt and worrying about everything that when the female officer walked into the interview room with another officer, I jumped out of my skin.

I was scared I was about to be in a whole lot of trouble for murdering Darren, yet it seemed so unfair because I was the victim of horrific circumstances, not him.

Maybe I was best making out I didn't know where Darren was, but I didn't think I'd make a convincing liar, so I vowed to tell them the truth, no matter the circumstances.

"Hello, my name is PC Andrews, but you can just call me John, I am from the Anti Kidnap and Extortion Unit here in the southwest of England. This is PC Tenner; they will be joining us today.."

"You can call me Amanda; I apologise for your wait." She said.

"How is my daughter?" I asked, she'd been in with Sandra for almost an hour, and I knew Hope could get very bored, very easily.

"She is fine, playing with a few toys in the room next door. She is happy Siobhan. We are more concerned for your wellbeing." The female officer tried to talk with me sympathetically.

"I am fine, I just want this to all be over with, so I can get back to my little girl."

"I am sure you do." John said before taking a seat. "We will try to not keep you too long."

John pulled out a file and Amanda explained that the interview needed to be recorded and asked if I gave my permission, I nodded my head.

"We need you to speak, as the recording can't detect a nod." She explained.

"Sorry, yes I agree."

"Can you please state your full name and date of birth name for me." Amanda asked.

"Siobhan Everdeen. The twenty fifth of November, nineteen ninety-seven."
"That makes you seventeen. Am I right?

"Yes that is right, eighteen at the end of the year." I explained.

"And you agree to this interview being recorded?"

"Yes."

"Okay Siobhan, can we go back to the very start, can tell me what happened the day you were abducted."

Hope's Interview

"Hope, my name is Sandra, can I ask you a couple of questions, will that be okay?" The lady asked me.

"Are you my new teacher?" I asked, "my mummy said when we get to the outside I can have a teacher."

The lady started to laugh at me, which made me laugh along with her. She had a happy smile like my mummy, but my mummy wasn't smiling that day.

"No, I'm not a teacher Hope, but I am here to make sure you are okay."

"I'm okay, but my mummy is sad." I looked down at the floor and noticed something colourful, "what is this?" I asked picking up one of the little box things.

"That is a Lego block."

"Lego?" It didn't look much like a leg.

"I am sure there are a lots of toys you haven't had the chance to play with. Do you have toys at mummy's house?"

"We don't have a house, not yet." I said and she asked me where we lived. "Once mummy gets help, we will be getting a real house with a fire and a home for Mr Spider."

I was happy and feeling excited because mummy and I would be moving into our Outside home soon. "Mummy said as soon as we get out of our room, she will get us a house."

"That sounds really lovely. Can you tell me about your old room?" she asked.

I told the lady about my Mr Christmas and all of our other drawings on the walls and how sometimes I saw colours on the same wall, but only if the sunshine was out to play. She smiled at me, and I smiled back.

"Where did you live before Hope?" The lady asked, but I was confused.

"With my mummy." I explained.

"Where with your mummy?" she asked.

"In our room, I just said that!"

It wasn't fun anymore, she kept asking me questions and I told her everything, but I just wanted to see my mummy. I didn't want to colour in anymore or talk to the smiley lady, I just wanted my mummy. When I told the lady I was finished colouring and I wanted to go back, she told me that I wasn't allowed. That upset me and I started to cry. It wasn't fair, my mummy promised me that she would always be with me, and when I wanted to see her, she wasn't there. That made me incredibly sad, and I no longer liked the lady talking to me, she reminded me of the nasty man from our room and I didn't like him much either.

"You are just like the nasty man!" I shouted and ran into the corner of the room.

"I didn't mean to upset you Hope, I am sorry." She said but I didn't want to talk to the lady anymore. "who is the nasty man?" she asked.

"I just want my mummy." I said turning my back on her.

CHAPTER TWENTY – Proving myself

You would have thought getting away from Darren was my biggest challenge, but it was starting to look like I needed to escape the law as well. I was convinced the female officer thought I was lying or hiding something because they'd had me held in that interview room for hours on end and nobody seemed to know what the hell was going on.

I was worrying about Hope and how she was dealing with everything because she had never spend time any away from me, even when Darren was in the room, Hope was still with me, just in the wardrobe, unseen but always there. I worried about how she was coping in a room full of strangers and no doubt being questioned just as intensely as I was.

Were they even allowed to question a little girl? I had no idea about law, and never thought I would have needed to know much about it either, but then again, it wasn't every day you'd escape the clutches of your abductor.

"Ms Everdeen, this is Mandy, she is a family liaison officer and is here to talk you through what is going to happen next. In the meantime, my colleague and I will investigate what you've told us so far. Is that okay?"

"Can I see my daughter now?" I asked for the tenth time.

"Very soon." Mandy responded, before taking the seat in front of me.

The woman started giving me all the usual crap about how they have mine and Hope's best interests at heart and I was listening to her in agreement until she had the nerve to tell me, the social services where worried for my daughters wellbeing, and they were in talks about whether or not Hope was better off with me, or whether it would be better placing her into emergency foster care while the police investigated my allegation further. *Allegation!* I was sure that was a word they used to say they didn't believe me. I was livid, who the hell did they think they were, my daughter was going nowhere without me.

"You are trying to take her off me!" I snapped, raising to my feet and ready to bolt it out the interview room.

"No one is trying to take Hope off you Miss Everdeen, it is just a temporary measure while the investigation is under way. You told the police some alarming information and until we know the facts, we need to do what is best for everyone involved." She looked at me and smiled, "that includes you Ms Everdeen."

"It's Miss!"

She looked at me like I had two heads. "I am not old enough to be a Ms."

"Sorry Miss Everdeen, I didn't mean to offend."

"Do you have any idea what I have been through?" I asked but the woman stayed silent. "No, you do not, so do not try and tell me what is best for me and my little girl! That in itself is offensive!"

"I can understand why you are upset..."

"Upset!" I started walking towards the door, to find out it was locked, "upset? You have no fucking idea how I feel." I found myself pacing the length of the small interview room, feeling just as trapped as I did with Darren. *Was this what being arrested was like?* "I am so fucking angry." I warned.

"I think it is best if you calm down Miss Everdeen, so we can talk about this in a calm manner." Mandy stood up and tried to come towards me.

"Don't you dare touch me!" I shouted, cowering to the floor like a beaten animal. I instantly started sobbing my little heart out.

***

Could they really take my daughter away from me?

The answer to that question was a resounding yes. It seemed they could do what the hell they wanted, and they clearly didn't listen to a word I had said. The day I was first interviewed Mandy asked me about my useless parents, and she asked me if I wanted them to be notified. I was over the age of sixteen and was told it was completely up to me, but I told them my parents had no right to know about my wellbeing, Mandy didn't understand why I was so cold about them and looked at me like a was some unruly teenage runaway. I tried to explain what my parents were like, but I guessed the woman had a brilliant upbringing herself and she no doubt had good parents because if she'd had any idea what mine were like, she wouldn't have gone behind my back and contacted them regardless.

    I was informed that the grandparents would be in consideration for a temporarily foster home for Hope. I made it abundantly clear to the social worker that I wasn't ready for my families involvement in any way, and I didn't even want them to know I was okay, never mind alive and had my own child. They probably wouldn't have cared about me in the slightest, but they would have happily corrupted my daughter. I wasn't ready to open that massive can of worms, but social services went against everything I had said. I was actually starting to feel like a convict and not the victim, but until the investigation proved my story, I was the main suspect.

***

    Within days the social services had made a call to the team who were based in Manchester to arrange for them to make a visit to my parents' house. Although, it was a complete waste of time and just as

Silent Hope | Sarah Louise Rosmond

I'd expected, it was deemed that my parents were not suitable to look after their granddaughter or any other child for that matter. My father was an alcoholic which I did inform them about his drinking problem when I was being questioned, but clearly I wasn't listened to. I even told them about the way he'd treated his kids and wife but there was no mention of my mum or of my siblings. I was told the social worker spoke to my father on his own which made me wonder if my parents were still together because the father I knew, wouldn't have let his wife or kids out of his sight. A lot could happen in five years, and I knew that more than most. Maybe my mother had finally left him, I really hoped that were the case.

The social worker hadn't told me much because of confidentiality laws, but she did make it clear, they didn't have any confidence that Hope would be looked after adequately and therefore she would have no choice but to keep Hope in a foster care home. I was assured it would be a provisional measure while the police investigation was underway.

I felt like a criminal myself, and I understood they needed to make sure my daughter was safe and well, but they had gone about it in all the wrong way as far as I was concerned, but who was I to talk, and who would listen to a teenage mum over a qualified social worker? I knew I didn't have a leg to stand on and as much as I disagreed with the way I was being treated, I constantly reminded myself that my daughter was safe, and well looked after and it wasn't going to be forever. Even if I had to prove myself as a mother, I was prepared to do everything in my power to give my baby girl the life she deserved.

After I was interviewed that first day, I was led into a room to see Hope before they took her away. My heart was breaking into a million little pieces, but I had to stay strong for my little girl. Hope was a little upset to find out she wasn't going to be staying with me for a while, but Sandra the social worker, done an excellent job in bribing my daughter with toys and treats, and my baby girl was lapping it up just like any four years old would. It was the excitement on her face and the thought of her having the opportunity of being a normal little girl, that made me agree to the stupid rules for contact.

Selfishly I wanted my baby girl with me, but she was being given the chance to see what a loving family home would look like, and I had promised her that opportunity since they day she could talk. It wasn't how I had it all planned in my head, but while I was still under investigation, it was the best thing I could have done for her. My heart broke at the thought of saying goodbye, but I knew it wasn't going to be forever. We both had the rest of our lives together, free do live the way we wanted to live, we just needed to get through all the rubbish bits first. We'd survived a hell of a lot worse while living with Darren and I knew we'd get through anything.

It was agreed that Hope was being homed with a local family who lived in the next town, the foster parents had a teenage son and a five-year-old daughter who they were already fostering, but they were keen to take in Hope and had a spare room all ready for her. I wasn't sure how my daughter was going to cope being in a bedroom on her own, and I voiced my concerns, only to be told they will inform the foster carers that she may be unsettled. I was then told social services had found me a room to stay in at a Woman's Aid refuge just outside of town and that I would be given my very own social worker who would be working alongside Sandra and Hope and keeping me in the loop. I was advised that the police would be in regular contact with me as the investigation got underway, so I needed to get myself a mobile phone as soon as I got chance to.

From all the information I was been given I knew it wasn't going to be a quick fix and I did worry what impact it was all going to have on Hope, at the end of the day, she was my main priority and always would be.

***

I was eventually awarded daily contact with my daughter, but that took almost a week to set up and I made a point of arguing with my own social worker daily, I honestly couldn't see why my daughter wasn't at the hostel with me, when the other mothers had their kids with them, I even had an empty bed in my room as a reminder that I was for the first time in five years, alone. I tried to put myself into everyone else's shoes and obviously when I first turned up at the police station, I could have been anyone, claiming to be the little girl's mother but the police's medical team had taken my blood and done a DNA test on us both myself and Hope, which came back confirming I was Hope's biological mother. What more proof did they want? I couldn't understand why they were keeping her away from me, it was unfair, and I made sure the whole staff knew how I felt, not in a moany way, but just asking a lot of questions and pestering them for any kind of updates.

I made sure they didn't think I was being awkward by agreeing to everything suggested, including attending parent groups and the mother's coffee mornings organised by Women's Aid. It was hard attending courses based around my child when my child was living over eight miles away from me.

***

Days turned into weeks really quickly, and before I knew it, three weeks had passed without any contact from the police. The last I had heard; they were searching for Darren. I had no idea whether the man was alive or if I did in fact leave him for dead. I should've cared, especially after everything he'd put me through, but he was the only person I had known for years. I hated him and pitied him all at the same time and I was angry at myself for even giving him a second of my time, but I was told that was part of my trauma response.

In order to see Hope twice a week, I was being forced to have counselling to determine whether or not I was responsible enough to have full custody of my own daughter. I was told that as long as I passed my evaluation Hope could finally live with me at the Woman's refuge. The refuge was meant to be a temporary fix, while the local council and social workers found us a house, but it didn't seem like anyone was doing anything to help find us a property. Which had me feeling a little more than frustrated, especially as I had seen a few empty houses locally while on my daily mental health walk, advised by my therapist. Oh, and I wasn't allowed to show any form of negative emotions, otherwise I didn't get to see my daughter that day. *Like how was that helpful in any way?*

I was in my therapy session one Monday afternoon and after hearing that Hope had come down with a cold, I was upset and annoyed that my visit was cancelled. I voiced my frustrations at Helena, my therapist but she went running straight back to the staff and before I knew it I was advised to start an anger management course. I didn't need to control my anger; I needed the whole ordeal to be over an done with. I felt less trapped in Darren's basement than I did with all those opinionated eyes on me, twenty-four hours a day.

One silver lining to it all was I had met a girl in the hostel, Megan, she was similar age to me, and she was also fighting the social services to get her son back. After leaving her abusive boyfriend she was placed in the hostel but within weeks of being there she had her little boy taken into care, as the staff believed she was struggling to cope with him. She was struggling, the woman had just left her abusive partner and was messed up, she gave that man everything, hoping he would revert back to the lovely bloke she once knew, but instead he destroyed her, and rather than the authorities helping to support her, they placed baby Joseph into temporary foster care to give her time to adjust and heal.

Megan had been in the hostel for just over a year when I first met her and she got to see her boy for a few hours daily, but it seemed unfair, the more I got to know about her and her story, the more I could relate and that started a friendship over mutual understanding. Her contact was originally set for once a week but over time it increased. You can imagine finding that out, had me worried about how long it would take to get out of that place myself. Megan hadn't a police investigation over her head either, so it didn't fill me with much confidence at all.

"I am seeing Joe today, and they said if the visit goes well again, I may be allowed to have him over night." Megan came back from her appointment excited and full of beans.

"That's amazing news, I am so happy for you both."

I was pleased for Megan, because all I'd witnesses was a survivor like myself and she was growing stronger and more confident as the weeks went on. A part of me was a little envious, I am not going to lie, but that was my own issue to deal with and not something I wanted to push onto my new friend, when things were finally going so well for her.

"It won't be long before they let Hope stay here with you too." Megan said, as if she knew what was going on in my mind.

"I do hope you're right, but I have a feeling, that is a long way off for me."

"Don't say that Von, you are an amazing mummy, look at all you both have been through, and you are still standing. I know I wouldn't have survived half of what you've had to endure. You should be proud."

Bless her, what a lovely thing to have said, but I didn't feel pride, I just felt useless. I wanted to give my baby girl the world and it was a far cry from the life I'd promised her.

Megan was a God send and without having someone to talk to, someone normal like myself, someone who also didn't have an easy run of things, made me feeling stronger willed. Knowing I had an ally and a friend, was comforting and gave me the inner fire I needed to carry on.

There were over twenty women living in the refuge, some of them were mummy's but most were single women, some in hiding from their ex-partners and others just found themselves homeless after leaving an abusive relationship. Either way, we were all there because a man had messed with us, one way or another. Which meant the hostel was a breeding ground for male hatred. Was hard not to look at the opposite sex negatively when everyone had a horror story to tell.

The only woman living there who was still in a relationship with her partner was Dakota, she was only placed in the hostel because of an issue with her claiming benefits. Originally from Poland, Dakota moved to England after falling in love with an Essex boy online, he promised her the world and she left everyone she knew in Poland to be with the man. Two daughters later and their relationship went sour when Dakota found him in bed with someone who was meant to be their friend. Dakota was heartbroken and moved back to Poland. From what I can gather, Poland was a dangerous place for her to bring up two girls on her own, so she came back to England and eventually she meant Thomas, the father of her baby girl, Olivia. Her boyfriend Thomas worked on the oilrigs and on one occasion while he was away for work, all of Dakota's money was stopped for her and the kids, unfortunately the poor woman had no way of feeding her daughters, not until Thomas returned home weeks later. Social services got wind of this through her daughters school, and Dakota was placed in the hostel. Thankfully, she was allowed to keep her girls with her, and watching her daughters playing around the communal kitchen, almost had me welling up at first but as time went on, I looked forward to the day that Hope got to meet them. Dakota's eldest Izabella was seven, and Zofia was the same age as Hope. I easily imagined Hope playing for hours on end and loving having someone her own size to play with.

All the women seemed lovely, although there was one woman who just rubbed me up the wrong way. I didn't smoke and never had, but I had an abrupt Irish woman asked me on the first day, if she could bum a cigarette off me. When I told her, I didn't smoke, she called me a liar and got it in her head, that I said no to her just to be spiteful.

After that day I would get a filthy look off her every time she saw me, and I was starting to worry that one day I might have wiped that smug little look off her face, but I knew I couldn't do anything, not while we all lived in the same building anyway.

It didn't help that I was already attending an anger management class, so the last thing I needed was to add to that by kicking Patricia's arse.

I told myself that I would get my chance with her one day, but only if she continued her hate campaign against me. Her little gang of two would snigger behind my back, but you could see Rachel was just a little lap dog, keen to lick Irish Pat's arse for her had she asked.

    I found I could ignore them most of the time. Some days it felt like I was back in primary school, and it was a lot of unnecessary grief, over a bloody cigarette.

CHAPTER TWENTY-ONE – Disappearing Darren

It had been a good six weeks before the police finally got back to me, and I found out they had been useless. It had taken them six weeks to basically do nothing. I wasn't able to provide them with an address to the house I was held captive in, obviously which made their job a lot harder, but I would have assumed the police had ways of finding all that type of stuff out on their own.

The woman who picked me and Hope up from the roadside was able to give a rough idea of where we were, but that was all it was, a rough idea as Hope and I had been walking for ages before we were picked up.

I didn't know whether or not they had looked into the crazy doctor either, I gave them so much information about the compound, everything that Darren had told me, as well as the information I personally knew but either they didn't take me seriously, or my information wasn't enough as nothing was mentioned. I worried they may not have believed me because surely they would have wanted to hurry it all along, they'd been told that other girls were involved, and they were in danger of being sold off. With no real rush to anything it was not wonder I questioned everything. I wanted so badly for it to all be over and done with and I voiced my concerned to my friend, Megan. She was my rock and I felt like I could talk to the girl about anything, but little did I know Irish Pat was listening in, that was all I needed.

I'd heard Patricia running her mouth off about me to her little lap dog and it took all my strength not to lash out at her. I was already in bad form and needed to get out for the afternoon before I did something I was going to regret. I needed to destress otherwise I would have taken out all of my frustrations out on Irish Pat's face, and that wasn't going to help my case. I hated being in that situation and the whole ordeal was made even harder living in the same building as Patricia, she was basically like my arch enemy at times.

What really made matters worse, was Megan had been told she would be moving out of the hostel and into her own place with Joseph as long as she carried on with her weekly meetings with Woman's Aid. I was upset as the prospect of losing my only friend in that place. It had been an exceptionally long time since I had been able to call anyone a friend and I knew I was going to miss her dearly.

Megan had talked me into finally buying a dreaded mobile phone, more so to keep me safe and so I had a way of calling for help if I needed it. I'm not sure what I had against the small handheld devices, but it took me weeks to buy one and I went for the cheapest option. I was saving up for when Hope was finally allowed to move in with me. I nearly didn't buy a phone but with Darren nowhere to be seen, I was on high alert. Not that I believed he would have been foolish enough to try and find me, not with the police out looking for him but I was still paranoid.

I had no idea if the man was dead or alive, whether or not I had left him injured or if he was on the run. Owning a mobile phone gave me a little bit of confidence to face the outdoors, otherwise I reckon I would have locked myself in that hostel and never came out.

The walk to the park only took me ten minutes, I must've been annoyed because it would normally take me a good twenty minutes to half an hour walking at a normal speed. The park was quiet, and I was grateful to just be away from everyone, everyone except for my baby girl.

I sat on the park bench, and I cried my heart out, I didn't care who could see or hear me, I just needed to get it all out of my system. I should have been grateful to be outside, with the sun on my skin and the wind in my hair, but I was broken without my daughter by my side, no matter how much I tried to be strong and brave for her, I wasn't sure how much more I could handle, I was hitting my breaking point and I knew it.

It had been months of investigations and months of jumping through hoops but finally the day came when Hope was allowed to stay with me fulltime and I couldn't have been happier. I had it all planned out, and the staff at the hostel were more than supportive and let me move into a bigger room, so Hope and I had more space.

I'd been out and grabbed a few things for us, excited for our first night in our new room together and it felt good knowing that the money I was receiving off the government was being used on things we needed, and I didn't have to beg or preform sexual acts to get them. We had popcorn and chocolate, and I was excited to share those first moments with my daughter, after promising her that experience for so long. I was excited about being able to take her out, show her what a park was and play games with her.

That afternoon dragged, as I fantasied about all the things we could do together. I just couldn't wait to see her little face and give her the biggest hug ever. It was going to be lovely to spend more than an hour at a time with her, it seemed like things were going in the right direction.

My plans didn't go to plan at all because later that evening Hope was dropped off at the hostel by the social worker, who warned me that my daughter was incredibly quiet in the car and that she was more than likely ready for a sleep. I was gutted because I wanted our first night to be special, but Hope wasn't her normal self at all.

Months apart meant Hope had started to get used to living in a big house with a mummy and a daddy and having other kids around her, so her being forced to come back and live in a small room with me, wasn't anywhere near as exciting and Hope's behaviour showed that.

I had never known my child to be challenging or demanding, but that was how she turned up that evening, demanding I get her a drink, demanding I let her watch the television. Just being a complete spoiled brat and I wasn't about to let her get away with it.

"Excuse me, who do you think you are talking to Hope Everdeen, do I have to remind you how to be kind?" I asked.

"No!" She snapped.

I was shocked that my polite little girl was acting that way and as a punishment I told her she wasn't getting any of the treats I had for her.

"I don't care, I already had treats today. I want to go back to Carla's house." she said getting upset with me.

That cut me deep, even my own daughter didn't want to be with me. I was a failure, even to her.

I spoke to my counsellor during that first week and she'd explained that most children act up after spending time away from their parents and that it was completely normal for Hope to want all that luxury and comfort again, because it was just like going on holiday, and we all got holiday blues when we returned home. I didn't even want to explain I'd never had a holiday, so I couldn't relate, but what she'd said, made sense to me and I found myself taking less offence to Hope's outbursts. Thankfully, her attitude didn't last too long, and she was back to being my helpful, little sidekick within the week.

I found that a few of the adventures I had wanted to do with my daughter, she'd already had those first experiences with her foster family. It upset me at first, but we soon found a list of new and exciting things to do together and attending a swimming pool was on the top of our list. I wasn't a confident swimmer by any means and Hope had never been in a bath before. She'd even refused to have a bath at Carla's house because I used to wash her in the sink while we were living at Darren's and that was all she had ever known, so attending the swimmers was going to be interesting.

Megan and Joseph both joined us and even though we all spend most of our time in the small paddling pool, you could see Hope was keen to try and swim like the other kids in the bigger pool. She spent a lot of time observing the other kids and it was a weird feeling watching her, I felt proud of her but annoyed with myself for not trying to escape Darren's clutches a lot sooner.

"I want to swim mummy." Hope said, not taking her eyes off the bigger kids, playing in the main pool.

"We will teach you Jellybean. I will look into swimming lessons before we leave today if you want me to?" I asked.

"Yes please mummy, so I can be a mermaid like Chelsea?"

Chelsea was the foster parents youngest daughter who must have been about five years old, Hope loved her and said she was her absolute best friend, as well as Joseph. Even though Hope now lived with me, I arranged a weekly visit to her old foster families, so she didn't lose that bond with them. I promised my daughter she would be loved dearly by everyone in the outside world, and it was obvious that Carla was very fond of Hope.

"Just like Chelsea the mermaid, yes." I smiled at her, watching as her eyes lit up.

***

We said our goodbyes to Magen and Joseph before we started making our way back to the hostel. The whole walk home Hope was pointing out different things and asking me what they were called. She was so inquisitive which I usually loved that about her but then she pointed to a man with a darker complexion and asked me if the man needed a wash because he looked dirty. I wanted the ground to open up and swallow me whole, I didn't know where to put myself and apologised to the man who had overheard our conversation.

Thankfully, he didn't take any offence, he just smiled and said kids were curious little creatures and told me he'd been asked far worse questions in the past. I smiled awkwardly at the man, embarrassed and slightly mortified and then I looked down at Hope. The innocent look on her face was a picture and before I knew it we were both in fits of giggles. Once the man was out of earshot, I took the opportunity to explain different races to my daughter. Knowing we lived in a multicultural part of the world; it seemed only fair she knew as much as possible before attending any local clubs or starting school.

    The only downside to having Hope back with me, was my instinct to protect her was intensified and my mind had starting to play tricks on me. I was convinced at least once that I saw Darren stood at the bus stop opposite the women's refuse. I told myself I was being paranoid and with the police still in the dark about his whereabouts I had a valid reason to feel a little paranoid.

***

    That evening after speaking to the police over email and just making them aware of my possible sighting of Darren, I was informed that the officer heading my case would be in touch with me to arrange a meeting. The team had finally found the house I was kept in for over four years and wanted to ask me a few more questions. I was a little apprehensive but also relieved because there was now proof I was abducted and held captive. Although, there was still no sign of Darren, and the house was the last place I'd seen him, they would have found blood of Darren's at least in the entrance to mine and Hope's room and I wondered if that was the reason they needed to question me again. I had admitted to there being a fight with Darren on the day I escaped, they knew that because both Hope and I were covered in his blood.

    No one was ever going to say it to my face, but when I first turned up at the police station, I could tell they weren't all that convinced with my story. They had no suspects apart from myself, and up until that point, they didn't even have a crime scene. At least they would have seen the way in which Darren had us living and that would collaborate a lot of what I put in my original statement.

My altercation with Darren was in self-defence, but if a body was found, then I was sure I was going to be prosecuted for manslaughter at least. I killed a man no matter which way you looked at it, and that was the polices mindset too, I was sure of it.

***

"Thank you for coming in to see us Miss Everdeen." The police officer said, as she reached out her hand to shake mine.

"I heard you have some evidence?" My solicitor asked.

"Yes we do," she said, "as you are aware, we have located the property you told us about but unfortunately we haven't found the man you mentioned."

"So, no dead body?" I asked feeling relieved and scared all at once.

"No, I am sorry, but we did get blood samples and other forensic evidence which is being looked at as we speak."

"Okay, is that a good thing?" I turned to ask my solicitor who assured me it was. "What do you want with me?" I asked the police officer.

"We need to go through your statement again and just clarify a few things." She said, "I won't take up much of your time, I promise you."

CHAPTER TWENTY-TWO – The Investigation

Over the course of three months the police found more and more evidence to collaborate with my story. They had also found out some interesting information about my parents and how they never even reported me missing back when I was thirteen years old. What type of human being just ignores their child's disappearance? Mine obviously. With no information about my abduction, all they could go on was reports from myself and my four-year-old daughter. Oh, and Hope's father, who I had only just started dating weeks before my abduction. John had no idea what had happened to me, and he never told anyone about my abduction as he feared he'd be in trouble for even hanging out with Kelvin and the rest of our group. He soon forgot about that fateful day as my name was never really mentioned. I may as well of been invisible to everyone back then, so my disappearance went unnoticed.

The police told me that my father was questioned as part of the investigation, again no mention of my mother, and in a statement my father said I had ran away from home and he assumed I was with his estranged family. My father had never spoken, or even mentioned any of his family while I was growing up, so there was no chance in hell, I would have been staying with them, but the rest of the town weren't to know that and just took the man's word for it.

I knew my father hated me, he made that very obvious, but it hurt me to realise that my own mother didn't try and find me either. Maybe it was easier for her with me out of the picture.

It took some digging on a social media site, but I eventually found out my mother did end up leaving my father, and it looked like she moved to Spain two years after my abduction and has been hard to locate since. It didn't look like she'd been online for ages making it harder to find anything out about her. I couldn't blame my mother for being in hiding, after all my father had threatened her on numerous occasions that he'd track her down and kill her if she ever dared to leave him.

Back when I was about eight, my mother gave birth to my little brother and I remember a few weeks later, her attempting to leave my dad, but he found out and followed us to the train station and whatever was said to her, he made her change her mind and return home to him. That was the only attempt I knew about, but my father never let her live it down, hence the constant threats. As much as he was mainly all mouth, I was never entirely sure how much I could put past the man, he wasn't a humane person in anyway and that showed in the way he treated his wife and kids. He liked like we were the worst thing on the planet. Knowing he lived alone in a shitty little bedsit, made me smile to myself. He didn't deserve the family he had, and it seemed he had eventually lost us all.

***

The day came that I had been waiting for, they finally found Darren, or should I say Matthew McBryan. After the investigation led the police to the house I'd been held captive, details about the two men who abducted me emerged and it opened up a massive investigation as it wasn't just myself that had escaped and come forward. I honestly believed the police thought I had made the Russian doctor up because of the way they continued to question me about her.

Every other day I was back down at the station, either adding to my statements or answering questions but thankfully my solicitor was amazing and helped me through the entire process. At one point I was convinced I was being charged for wasting police time, but my solicitor backed my corner and pushed for the investigation to continue.

It was a few days later when the police located the house and forensics teams found DNA which proved my story and the blood-stained floor from the day we escaped proved the identity of my abductor. Matthew McBryan was already known and wanted by the police for a different investigation, but the man had been in hiding for over ten years.

I did wonder if it had anything to do with the disappearance of Helen, whoever she was. The police refused to talk about the other case as it wasn't anything to do with my own, which I understood, although I was frustrated that I didn't have all of the answers.

Finding out that Matthew had been arrested while trying to leave the country meant I could walk around without looking over my shoulder every second, and I was able to let go of the thought that I might have killed a man, even if it were in self-defence. It was premeditated and it could have easily been seen as murder, but the man was alive, injured and recovering but he was alive and caught trying to run away from his crimes. I was advised that the police would be busy building a case and I would be contacted in the near future with a court date. Thankfully, I wouldn't have to testify in the courtroom and all of my statements would be done via a video link, so I would never have to see Darren or should I say, Matthew's face ever again.

    My solicitor told me he was looking at a long sentence, but it wouldn't be as harsh as he admitted to buying me illegally and holding me captive. He refused to give any details about Anouska, the Russian doctor. The man did admit to killing his own son, which the police had no reason to look into until they read my original statement. With abduction and murder over his head, Darren was looking at spending the majority of what life he had left, rotting behind bars.

CHAPTER TWENTY-THREE – The Verdict

Eighteen months was how long I waiting to hear the words 'Guilty' from the judges mouth. Eighteen months of going back and forth, giving more and more statements, and answering questions. At times, the whole thing was so time consuming that I felt like I was missing out on Hope's upbringing. All the grand ideas I had about the life I wanted to give her, went out of the window because my poor girl spent more time with a social services recommended childminder, than she did with me, her own mother. If I wasn't at court, I was attending local pointless Women's Aid courses and seeing my therapist once a week too. I felt like I was missing her growing up and I was only really getting to spend time with her in the evenings, when she was overtired from all the fun adventures she'd been experiencing during the day.
I was a little jealous that a woman who was linked to social services was gaining a better bond with my daughter, than I was. So, the week of the court case I promised myself I would spend every waking hour with my daughter. I wanted us to go back to how we used to be, without obviously the restrictions of our captivity.

I was told that I didn't need to go to court the day of Matthew's sentencing, but I needed to, for my own sanity. I needed to watch him being led away so I could attempt to let go of that hold the man still had over me.

I've since been told I have a form of Stockholm Syndrome as Matthew was the only person I had known for years on end and the only person who actually wanted me because let's face it, my parents really didn't give a shit about me did they. Matthew abused me for years; in ways I haven't gone into details about because I am still not ready to completely open those wounds and yet I still felt a sadness for the man.

I felt a weird sense of guilt that I had spoken to the police about him, it was my faut he was facing the rest of his life behind bars because of the statements I had made. It was the biggest mind fuck ever and it hurt and confused me. I didn't even fully understand why I cared so much. He was a sick and vile creature, but he was all I had known for so long. That was where the Stockholm syndrome came into play, and the main reason why I needed therapy once a week.

Therapy helped me so much that I also got my daughter to attended an art therapy class, but Hope didn't ever show any signs of Stockholm syndrome because to her, living in a room with her mummy was the most normal thing in the world to do.

Even with her own bedroom in our new council house, Hope would opt to sleep in my bed, with me and when she felt a little anxious, I would find my little girl playing with her Bratz dolls in the bottom of her build in wardrobe. Other than that, Hope was your typical little girl with a zest for life and a sponge for knowledge. I was so grateful that the first part of her life, didn't mess her up too badly, as for me, that was another story.

***

The day we moved out of the hostel was the best feeling I had ever experienced. I thought I'd tasted freedom when Hope and I first escaped captivity, but I never really knew what it felt like until I was handed the keys to our two bedroomed apartment. The realisation creeped in just after I'd signed the tenancy agreement, the landlord left Hope and I standing in the empty living room on our own.

For the first time in my life, I had no one turning off the electric and no one having control over our food. For the first time in months, I had no staff watching over my every move, making sure I wasn't going to slip up or questioning my parenting. There was no one, just my little girl and me. That excitement soon turned into fear as I worried about how we'd cope, just the two of us.

As much as I hated living at the hostel, I had started to make friends and the staff as much as they did my head in, they all rallied around for me when they heard we were moving into our very our own place.

I was extremely fortunate as our little two bedroomed apartment was semi-furnished, which saved us a lot of money because I didn't need to folk out hundreds of pounds for a cooker, washing machine or a fridge freezer. I was also awarded a grant as it was my first property in the area and with the savings I'd made while being at the hostel we had enough money to buy Hope everything she had ever dreamed of for her new bedroom. She picked out a lovely pink princess four poster bed and a matching chest of drawers. It was an expensive set, but I wanted to treat her, after everything we'd been through, I felt it was the least I could do.

    I had spent the first three nights staying up until the early hours, decorating her bedroom, but Hope hated the thought of sleeping on her own, and asked if we could move her bed into my room. It was a bit of a squeeze, but we managed to make room and Hope's bedroom became her playroom instead. I didn't really mind as I was used to her sleeping with me from an early age, if anything I found it comforting.

    Our social worker on the other hand, didn't agree with the way I raised my daughter and told me I should have put my foot down and tried to persuade Hope into sleeping in her own room. I explained why my daughter felt more comfortable in bed with me, but she said my daughter needed that independence. The woman didn't know my daughter and she had no right telling me how I should raise her. It seemed like every time I had a visit from the social worker, they found something else to argue with me about. Although arguing with them didn't help me, if anything it meant even more home visits from them and eventually core meetings.

    During one of the visits, I disagreed with what my social worker was telling her boss that Hope was placed on the 'At Risk' register all because my social worker didn't like that I answered her back. I honestly believe that she hated the fact she couldn't bully me, she seemed like a bully, a woman with no kids of her own, but thought she had all of the answers.

I was annoyed understandably at first because there was zero risk to my daughter, not anymore and I believed letting her get used to the real world in her own time was the best option but apparently to them it was deemed as bad parenting. I really didn't care what they thought of me, when I knew I was doing what was best for my little family and apart from keeping a close eye on me, they had nothing they could use against me. When Hope was first placed on the register, I was threatened by the head of their department, that Hope could be placed into foster care again if they felt her needs weren't being met, unfortunately for them, I was meeting my child's every need, and more so.

My own social worker might not have been able to stand me, but her boss was lovely and if there was anything I disagreed with, or I needed help, I would go straight over my social workers head, and talk to her boss, Rebecca. As much as I didn't like all of the appointments and meetings, placing me under the spotlight felt a lot safer. Knowing I had social services around me, watching my every move was kind of comforting. It was hard not to be a little paranoid when you'd been through so much trauma, and I guessed I'd always be wary of others. My walls were up, but for good reasons.

***

Life settled down pretty quicky once we had our own little place and Hope was so excited to be starting the same school as both Megan son and Dakota's girls.

Silent Hope | Sarah Louise Rosmond

We'd got her prepared by attending the local youth clubs for her age group and just like I always imagined, Hope was friends with every single child who attended. She really thrived off being around other kids her own age and I was in ore watching her, because at one point, it was just a dream I had for her, which was now our reality.

It was the day before Hope's first day of school and because Joseph and Hope were going into the same reception class, Megan agreed to stay overnight. Megan would only stay over at the weekends, because of school, but that Sunday evening, she had no excuse to go home. Hope asked if she could have her bed back in her own bedroom because Joseph had his own room, Hope said she wanted to be a big girl. Megan and I spent half an hour sorting her room out. Hope was excited to show Joseph all of her toys, so we left them to it.

I was surprised when I checked on the kids ten minutes later, and Hope was fast asleep on her bed, Joseph was awake but didn't look like he was going to be awake for long.

Once we knew both the kids were settled, Megan poured us both out a well-deserved glass of wine. I didn't enjoy drinking wine at all, but I did enjoy the way it made me feel and Megan was more comical with a glass of wine in her. I would have never got drunk, but I did enjoy being tipsy.

"Both the kids are fast sleep, finally." I had just been in and checked on them.

"Drink?" Megan asked as I walked back into my living room.

"Of course, does a bear shit in the woods?"

Megan walked over to the table in front of the window and just stood there, looking outside into the dusky night sky. When I asked her what was wrong she said she didn't know.

"I think you have a visitor," she said, "someone is stood in the middle your driveway."

"What?" I said walking towards my window to have a look myself.

I couldn't make out who it was at first, but then they starting approaching the front of the house, it couldn't be.

"How did they find me? The police said I was safe!" I was scared and with good reason.

The end….. For now.

About the Author

Sarah Louise Rosmond

Firstly, I would like to thank you from the bottom of my heart for reading my book. I am well known for my best selling novel *My Life in His Hands* © I have had a rough time of things but all the obstacles in my life, became the fighting force behind my writing. After writing books about myself for so long it was so nice to delve more into my imagination to bring you new and exciting stories which will leave you feeling like you been living inside the storylines and eager to keep those pages turning. Silent Hope is a fiction novel with small elements of truth in it. I am excited to share this new series with you.

You can find more about me by following my social media accounts. I aim to reply to every message I receive. Your loyalty means the world to me, so, thank you once again and if you don't mind, leaving a review as it will help other readers find my books easier in the future.

Much Love Sarah xoxo

Printed in Great Britain
by Amazon